# ANNIE'S LIFE IN LISTS

## ALSO BY KRISTIN MAHONEY

*The 47 People You'll Meet in Middle School*

# ANNIE'S LIFE IN LISTS

## Kristin Mahoney

### Illustrated by Rebecca Crane

A YEARLING BOOK

Text copyright © 2018 by Kristin Mahoney
Cover art and interior illustrations copyright © 2018 by Rebecca Crane

All rights reserved. Published in the United States by Yearling,
an imprint of Random House Children's Books, a division of
Penguin Random House LLC, New York. Originally published
in hardcover in the United States by Alfred A. Knopf, an imprint of
Random House Children's Books, New York, in 2018.

Yearling and the jumping horse design are registered trademarks
of Penguin Random House LLC.

Visit us on the Web! rhcbooks.com

Educators and librarians, for a variety of teaching tools,
visit us at RHTeachersLibrarians.com

The Library of Congress has cataloged the hardcover edition
of this work as follows:
Names: Mahoney, Kristin Mary, author. | Crane, Rebecca, illustrator.
Title: Annie's life in lists / Kristin Mahoney ; Illustrated by Rebecca Crane.
Description: First edition. | New York : Alfred A. Knopf, 2018. |
"This is a Borzoi book." | Summary: Fifth-grader Annie
writes lists to keep track of changes in her life when her family
moves from Brooklyn to the small town of Clover Gap.
Identifiers: LCCN 2017003446 | ISBN 978-1-5247-6509-5 (hardcover) |
ISBN 978-1-5247-6510-1 (hardcover library binding) |
ISBN 978-1-5247-6511-8 (ebook)
Subjects: | CYAC: Lists—Fiction. | Moving, Household—Fiction. |
Family life—New York (State)—Fiction. | Friendship—Fiction. | Schools—
Fiction. | New York (State)—Fiction.
Classification: LCC PZ7.1.M34674 Ann 2018 | DDC [Fic]—dc23

ISBN 978-1-5247-6512-5 (paperback)

Printed in the United States of America
10 9 8 7 6 5 4 3 2 1
First Yearling Edition 2020

FOR MY THREE GREAT LOVES

WHELAN

LUCY
♡
ALICE
♡

**Five things I hate about my real name, Andromeda**

-------------------------------------------------------------------

1. Everyone says, "That's a weird name."

2. No one knows how to spell it.

3. No one knows how to pronounce it. (You pronounce it like this: "Ann-drama-duh.")

4. No one can remember it. (This one probably bothers me most, because *I* remember just about everything.)

5. Even though most people call me Annie, my brother says my nickname should be Drama or Duh. (His name is Ted, after my great-grandfather. Apparently, Mom and Dad saved all their naming flair for me.)

**Three things I like about my name**

-------------------------------------------------------------------

1. My mom says I was named after her favorite constellation.

2. My dad says Andromeda was also a mythical princess.

3. My nickname, Annie

I am Annie. This is my life in lists.

## Nine things I see when I look in the mirror

1. Freckles. Lots of them. Especially in summer, of course.

2. Indescribable hair color. Not indescribable like "indescribably beautiful!" Just really hard to describe. Not blond. Not brown. My Grandma Elaine calls it "dirty blond," but I don't like the sound of that.

3. Green eyes (my favorite part)

4. A bump on the bridge of a long nose (This I get from my mom.)

5. A little gap between my two front teeth

6. Almost always: a T-shirt

7. Almost always: leggings or jeans

8. In summer: flip-flops

9. In winter: sneakers or boots

## Three things I never see when I look in the mirror

1. A dress

2. Expensive sneakers (My mom doesn't "believe" in them.)

3. Smooth hair (It's always kind of straggly, even five minutes after I've brushed it.)

### Three things you can't tell just by looking at me

1. I'm left-handed (although if you looked really closely, you might see that I always have pencil smudges on my left pinky from where my hand has dragged across my writing).

2. I'm allergic to amoxicillin.

3. I have an amazing memory.

### Five things about my memory

1. I have a regular memory for things like spelling tests and phone numbers.

2. I have a not-so-great memory for things like bringing permission slips back to school and putting my homework folder in my backpack.

3. I definitely do not have a crime-solving photographic memory like Cam Jansen.

4. I have a weirdly amazing memory for things about people. I remember their names, what they wore on different days, who their brothers and sisters are, what their houses look like, and what their pets are named.

5. I remember things about people that they will never remember about me. In fact, there are kids at my school who don't even know I exist, but I could tell you their names, their favorite sports, where they went on vacation, and what they ate for lunch.

## Four things other people say about my memory

1. My mom says it runs in the family, and that some people just have amazing memories. (Hers is pretty good too. She remembers the names of all my grandparents' cousins, even on my dad's side. And her old friends tell her she's like their "childhood Google," because anytime they forget something from when they were kids—the name of a teacher, the secret nicknames they had for their crushes, the ending of a crazy story—they just ask her.)

2. My dad says I should be proud of how much I remember.

3. My best friend, Millie Lerner, thinks it's cool because:

    a. I can tell her the names of all the fifth-grade boys she thinks are "interesting."

    b. I remember all the teachers' first names (from reading the PTA directory one day while I was bored).

    c. When someone annoys her, I make her feel better by reminding her of embarrassing things they did when they were younger. (For example, when Millie got glasses, Hannah Krenzler called her a four-eyed freak and I told Millie not to sweat what Hannah says, because she used to shove her teddy bear's fur up her nose.)

**4.** Ted says my memory is creepy and makes me seem like a stalker.

I tell him you would not believe how much you would learn if you just paid attention. But Ted still has a habit of nudging me when he thinks I'm going to say too much. Especially when I'm remembering something about him and someone in his grade. *Especially* if it's a girl. (Like when we saw Sophia Karlin in Key Food and I reminded him of how he once said she looked like Queen Amidala. He stepped on my toe for that one. Hard.)

**What I think of my memory**
---------------------------------------------------------------------

1. I won't admit this to Ted, but it *can* be a little embarrassing. Remembering so much about people can make you feel like no one else is as interested in you as you are in them. For example:

   a. Once, Millie and I knocked on her neighbor Sheila's door to tell her we'd found her cat in the hallway. Sheila's son Pete had been on Ted's soccer team three years earlier, and all the boys called him Professor because he was always sharing weird soccer trivia that no one else knew. Of course I remembered this, so when Pete answered the door I automatically said, "Hey, Professor. We found Mittens." He squinted at me for a second before saying, "Who are *you*?"

So to recap, not only did I know his nickname *and* his cat's name, but he had no idea who I was. Even though I had been at every one of his soccer games. And he had come to the team pizza party at our apartment. And I was his neighbor's best friend. You'd think *he* might be embarrassed not to know *me,* but somehow I was the one who was blushing.

b. On the first day of school last year, when my teacher, Ms. Allen, wondered aloud how we would distinguish between the two Emmas in our class since both of their last names started with "S," I said, "We could just call one Emma Marie and the other Emma Elizabeth." Because I remembered both of their middle names. From when they had them written on their plastic Easter baskets at an egg hunt in the park. In kindergarten. Clearly neither Emma remembered this, though, because they both looked at me and said, "How do you know my middle name?" in stereo. Cue red face again.

2. Lately, it's a serious problem. Since my memory got me kicked out of school, Ted really doesn't have to worry anymore about me saying too much. Now I keep all this information to myself.

**Four things I have pretended not to remember so people wouldn't think I was weird**

---

1. The first, middle, and last name of a kid I met once at a birthday party when I was in kindergarten, four years ago (and the fact that he didn't want ice cream, and that he completely missed the donkey in Pin the Tail on the Donkey)

2. A conversation I had with Jesse Bruner in first grade where he told me he hadn't washed his hair in two months

3. The street my teacher lives on

4. The names of people who don't know *me,* when I see them in public, like when Aidan Little from my old kiddie music class was standing right in front of Mom and me in line at the movies. Or when Lola Moran, one of the leads in the school musical, put her blanket down beside ours at a summer concert in the park. (I didn't just pretend not to know their names; I pretended not to notice they were there at all. It wasn't that hard since they didn't notice me, either. And I don't think they were pretending.)

Anyway, it's not such a big deal for me to lie low like I did with Aidan and Lola, because I'm a pretty quiet kid anyway.

## Four examples of how quiet I can be

1. On my third day of day camp last summer, the head counselor marked me absent because she didn't notice I was there.

2. Whenever it was time to line up in preschool, my teacher would say, "Let's see who else can be as quiet as Annie." (Mom put a stop to that one after I told her about it.)

3. Our neighbor across the hall, Mrs. Hartzell, called me "Angie" for a year, and I never spoke up. (Ted finally corrected her when he heard her say it.)

4. In second grade, Charlotte Devlin made me give her my peanut butter crackers every day at lunch. Peanut butter crackers are my favorite, but I never told anyone. Toward the end of the year, Millie noticed this was happening, and she told Charlotte to cut it out. That's how Millie and I became friends.

## Four reasons I'm quiet

1. I'm listening.

2. I'm watching.

3. I'm thinking.

4. I don't know what to say.

The last one happens a lot. I see other people joke about things they've done together, but if I bring up something I remember about someone, I'm afraid she'll think I'm weird for remembering it. Or, in the case of Charlotte and the peanut butter crackers, I'm afraid someone won't like me. So instead I don't say anything.

### One unique situation where I wind up talking too much

1. When I'm nervous and the only other person in the room is an adult. Especially an adult with authority. I'm not sure why I do it. Maybe I think that if I talk enough, I'll be able to keep whatever it is that I'm nervous about from happening.

I know this doesn't make me special. Lots of kids probably babble when they wind up one-on-one with a teacher or a coach. Or their school principal. But most kids don't have the same memory I have. So their babbling isn't such a big deal.

### One time my memory—and my babbling—turned out to be a very big deal

1. When I told the principal, Mr. Lawrence, that his brother looked like a dry cleaner

## Nine reasons I was nervous in front of Mr. Lawrence

1. I had never been to his office before. (Being a quiet, cooperative kid, I'm not the sort of person who finds herself getting sent to the principal very often. Or ever.)

2. He was the principal. (See above: adults in authority make me nervous.)

3. I was delivering a note from my teacher, Mrs. Simmons.

4. I had no idea what the note was about.

5. My imagination was starting to run a little wild as I wondered what the note might say.

6. I wondered if it had something to do with *The Pinballs,* a book I'd borrowed from Mrs. Simmons's classroom library and never returned because I lost it.

7. I wondered if the note was Mrs. Simmons asking Mr. Lawrence what my punishment should be.

8. Then I wondered if the note was something good, like a request for a class party. Or a field trip. Or an award for the most cooperative student.

9. Wait . . . maybe that last one wasn't actually good. An award for cooperation would just be embarrassing, really.

Anyway, you see where my nerves were coming from. So while I waited for Mr. Lawrence to read the letter, I began to babble.

**What I babbled about in Mr. Lawrence's office**

1. His pictures. Really just one picture. Specifically, a framed photo of him and another man that I spied on his cabinet.

2. I said, "Excuse me, Mr. Lawrence, but who is the man in that picture?" He told me it was his brother, and I said, "He looks just like the dry cleaner on my block."

3. Mr. Lawrence said, "Are you sure?" And I answered, "Yes. He has a cat named Oliver who always sits on the counter. We went there once a long time ago to get my dad's jacket cleaned, but when the jacket came back my dad's eyes got all watery, and Mom said she thought there was cat hair on it, and my dad is allergic. So we go to a different dry cleaner now."

**Six reasons that was a bad idea**

---

1. Mr. Lawrence said, "My brother is a dry cleaner, and he has a cat named Oliver. But his store isn't in this neighborhood."

2. I didn't live in that neighborhood either.

3. Mr. Lawrence asked, "You say my brother's dry-cleaning shop is on the block you live on now?"

4. I tried to say yes, but no sound came out.


What Mr. Lawrence didn't know was that my family had moved years ago when I was in preschool because the rent went up on our old apartment. According to the city's rules, Ted would have been allowed to stay in that school, but I wouldn't have been guaranteed a spot there when I started kindergarten, especially because the space was really limited. Since my parents wanted me to be able to go to the same school as Ted, they didn't tell anyone about our move. The new tenants in the apartment put any mail addressed to us—including letters from the school—on a table in the entryway, and we stopped by every once in a while to pick it up.

Mom and Dad kept saying we'd move back to the old neighborhood eventually, once we could afford it again. And they told Ted and me not to say anything about it at school. They said it didn't matter since we would move back soon, but the Department of Education might not understand that.

But Dad never got the raise he was hoping for at work, and he and Mom seemed more worried about money than ever, so we stayed put.

5. Where we used to live in Brooklyn, school zoning is a pretty big deal. Suddenly my face felt very warm, and my stomach felt like a squirrel was trapped inside it. I knew I had blown our cover.

6. The cat was out of the bag. (And sitting right on the dry cleaner's counter.)

I never did find out what was in the note Mrs. Simmons sent to Mr. Lawrence.

**Five things that happened after the dry cleaner incident**

1. Mr. Lawrence called my parents and asked if we had moved.

2. Mom and Dad fessed up.

3. Mr. Lawrence said I could finish the school year there, but that I would have to switch schools in the fall.

4. Mom and Dad started having lots of quiet talks in their room with the door closed. (Once, I overheard Dad saying, "How does she even remember that dry cleaner? We haven't used them in years!" And Mom said, "We can't let her think this is her fault.")

5. On the last day of school, they hit Ted and me with big news: Dad had gotten a new job working as an engineer on a big highway project, and that summer we were going to move to Clover Gap, a teeny town about seven hours away from the city.

**Three ways my family reacted to the news about the move**

1. Ted started spending every free minute at his friend Joe's house. And when he was home, he was usually in his room with the door closed and music blaring.

2. Mom cleaned out every closet and drawer and gave away anything we hadn't used in the past six months. I had to keep a close watch on her to make sure she didn't toss anything important.

3. Dad stayed home from work a lot more than usual. During the day he helped Mom with cleaning, and at night he was always online, researching things he was going to have to know for his new job. He seemed a little nervous about it. I guess building a new highway in the country is a lot different from the kinds of projects he did in the city. But he also talked constantly about how awesome life in Clover Gap was going to be, and all the cool things we would do there. (Hike in the woods! Canoe in the lake! Roast marshmallows in our own backyard!)

**Five ways I reacted to the news about the move**

1. "What?!" My family had lived in Brooklyn since before I was born. Mom and Dad sometimes talked about wanting a house and a big yard, but I never thought they'd actually do something about it. And now, all of a sudden, we were moving so far away?

2. Worrying. What would the other kids be like? Would anyone want to be friends with me? How would I survive without Millie? Would anyone there be as great as her? And how would life in the country be different? Would there be more bugs? What about bears?

3. Wondering.

When I overheard Mom saying, "We can't let her think this is her fault," what did that mean? That she really thought it *was* my fault that we were going to move, and she just didn't want me to feel bad about it? Did Dad have to get a new job because of me? (I mean, wasn't it weird that he happened to get a new job right when I blabbed to Mr. Lawrence?)

Also, I wondered what the deal was with Dad's new job. Mom's job is pretty flexible—she's a graphic designer, and she can work from home. But would Dad still have work once the highway was finished? And if not, did that mean we'd get to move back to Brooklyn? When I asked about that, Dad sighed and Mom just said, "One thing at a time, Annie. One thing at a time." So I'm still wondering.

4. Wishing I'd kept my big mouth shut with Mr. Lawrence

5. Waiting for Ted to stop hating me


**Six ways Ted and I used to spend time together**

1. Watching TV

2. Arguing

3. Washing dishes. This was our job every night after dinner: I washed and Ted dried. I tried to get him to take turns (I hated washing every night because my fingers got pruney and I never felt like I could get the pots clean enough), but he said he was the only one tall enough to reach the high shelves to put the glasses away, so he had to be the dryer until I got taller.

4. Building Dixie Cup towers. We'd done this since we were little. Ted would probably have been embarrassed to admit that we still spent as much time on this as we did (he knocked them down if one of his friends was coming over), but we were really good at it. We built towers that were taller than my dad.

5. Watching YouTube videos about wild animals. Some of these were really cute, like the ones with mama elephants and their babies. But one day Ted stumbled across a video of a bear attacking a guy who was making a wildlife documentary.

I will spare you the details, but let's just say I had nightmares for a month. And Ted got in big trouble for showing it to me.

6. Listening to music. When he was in a good mood, he'd ask me to listen to new music he liked, then make playlists of my favorites and put them on my iPod. So I had playlists with names like

   a. Annie's Jams (music that made me happy)

   b. Annie Dances (music to dance to, obviously)

   c. Settle Down, Sister (songs to listen to when I was angry)

**Four reasons I suspected Ted was angry about the move**

1. Even though I was going to have to go to a different school if we stayed in Brooklyn, his life would have barely changed. (He's twelve and in middle school, and for him it didn't matter what neighborhood we lived in.)

2. He had his heart set on applying to LaGuardia, a really famous performing arts high school in Manhattan, next year.

3. His classic-rock cover band, Ted Zeppelin (the band name was always changing, but that was the latest one), had finally booked some "gigs" for the summer.

4. He yelled, "Why couldn't you keep your stupid

mouth shut?!" when he heard the story about Mr. Lawrence and the dry cleaner.

So I guess I more than *suspected* Ted was angry about the move. I knew he was angry. It was pretty clear he thought it was all my fault, and I had a feeling he was right. It was because of my big mouth that we were moving.

**Three things I used to be known for at school**

1. Being a good writer

2. Being Millie's best friend

3. Never getting in trouble

I realize those aren't the most interesting things to be known for in fourth grade. It's not like being the fastest runner or the best artist, or having an uncle who's a movie star. So the truth is that a lot of people probably didn't know me at all. But that has started to change.

## One thing I'm now known for at school
-------------------------------------------------------------------------
1. Getting myself kicked out

I'm not sure how she heard, but a few days after my visit to Mr. Lawrence's office, Hannah Krenzler came up to me at recess and said, "Is it true that you aren't allowed to come back to school here next year?" When I told her my family was moving, she said, "I heard you got yourself kicked out." Just then the bell rang for us to go back inside, so I didn't have a chance to say more. But that was only the beginning.

## Five rumors that started about why I had to leave school
-------------------------------------------------------------------------
1. I walked into Mr. Lawrence's office and insulted his family.

2. I walked into Mr. Lawrence's office and broke something.

3. I walked into Mr. Lawrence's office and cursed.

4. I stole something from Mrs. Simmons.

5. I thought I was too smart for this place, and I was switching to a boarding school for quiet geniuses.

Every time I heard one of these rumors, I didn't even know what to say. They were so crazy. So I stayed quiet, as usual. I became quieter than I ever was before. And the quieter I got, the more people seemed convinced I was hiding a big secret. The more I tried to disappear, the bigger the stories about me got.

By the end of the school year, I felt like I never wanted to see most of my classmates again. Convenient, I guess, since I was about to move far away.

The only person I knew I would truly miss was Millie.

**Three things I thought Millie would say when I told her about the move**

1. You can't leave me!

2. You have to stay here!

3. If they make you leave, I will visit you every weekend!

**Three things Millie actually said when I told her about the move**

1. Your parents should never have lied in the first place.

2. But why did you have to spill the beans to Mr. Lawrence?

3. I can't believe you have to move because you got kicked out of school.

### Three things I said back to Millie

1. I didn't mean to tell Mr. Lawrence; it was a stupid mistake.

2. That's NOT why we're moving! It's because my dad got a new job. (I didn't tell her I was also starting to become convinced we were moving because of me.)

3. Everybody's parents lie about something. Yours have been telling you that you've had the same goldfish for years, and I can totally tell they switch it every time the old one dies!

This was kind of a bold move for me. Millie always told me how I was so "easy" (meaning agreeable, I guess), and it felt good to hear that. And I didn't mind so much that Millie was usually the one making plans and decisions for us; she had great ideas.

**Millie's three greatest ideas**

---------------------------------------------------------------

1. Second grade: crush leftover Halloween candy and sprinkle it into pancake batter (This was the morning after our first sleepover.)

2. Third grade: the Wildlife Warriors. As members of the Wildlife Warriors, we walked around Prospect Park looking for injured birds, squirrels, and chipmunks, and if we found one, we would call the Parks Department and report our discovery. We only ever found two animals in trouble (a bird that couldn't fly and a squirrel that appeared to be limping), and the Parks Department people sounded more amused than concerned, but Wildlife Warriors was still mostly fun.

3. Fourth grade: world's longest lanyard. After Millie learned how to make lanyards at camp, she had the idea that we'd get into the *Guinness Book of World Records* by making the longest lanyard ever. (We needed to figure out if there even *was* a longest-lanyard record . . . ours was only about three feet long. We weren't able to work on it as much as we wanted once our homework load picked up.)

Anyway, maybe it's weird for two people who were together as much as we were, but Millie and I had never had a fight. Even if her ideas weren't always ones I would have chosen (I got pretty tired of walking all over the park looking for hurt squirrels that didn't exist, and my fingers had blisters on them from so much lanyard-ing), it didn't seem worth it to start a disagreement. I always felt safe with her. Until now. Because after I yelled that bit about the fish, she clearly was not happy.

So now Millie was mad at me too (and not just at me, at my whole family). The list of things I felt guilty about was getting longer. Just to review:

**Five things I felt guilty about at the end of fourth grade**
------------------------------------------------------------

1. Exposing my parents as liars in front of the principal

2. Sharing a family secret that got me kicked out of my elementary school with just one year left

3. Taking my brother away from a promising high school musical career, and possibly derailing his musical aspirations for the rest of his life

4. Taking my brother away from his friends and his band

5. Unintentionally devastating my best friend by revealing that her goldfish was not who she thought he was

**One person who did not seem ready to forgive me anytime soon**
------------------------------------------------------------

1. Ted

I think he said about three words to me the entire summer.

## One person who did seem ready to forgive me
--------------------------------------------------------------
1. Millie

The night before she was leaving for summer camp, our buzzer rang. It was Millie, holding a whole case of peanut butter crackers.

## Three apologies Millie made as we snacked on peanut butter crackers in my room
--------------------------------------------------------------
1. I'm sorry I said that about your parents.

2. I'm sorry I didn't do more to stop the crazy rumors about you at school. I tried, but they took on a life of their own.

3. I'm sorry I got so mad when you told me about the goldfish. I kind of suspected it anyway.

## Two apologies I made
--------------------------------------------------------------
1. I'm sorry I said that about the goldfish.

2. I'm sorry I told Mr. Lawrence where I live. I didn't mean to, but I know I messed up.

Millie said I didn't have to apologize for that. She knew it was an accident.

I told her I thought we might get to move back to Brooklyn once Dad's highway job was over. She said, "Well, then I hope they work fast up there in the boonies."

## Four promises we made to each other

1. We would always be best friends.

2. We wouldn't let anyone else be our best friends.

3. We would make our parents let us visit each other.

4. We would write each other emails or letters all the time.

And that was it. Millie left early the next morning for camp. I wondered if saying goodbye was as weird for her as it was for me. She definitely seemed sad, but I was sad *and* more than a little scared. Like I said, I'd always felt safe with Millie. I don't think I realized just *how* safe until I started thinking about life without her.

Mom hadn't made any summer plans for me since we were moving, and I suddenly felt like the only kid left in Brooklyn.

## Seven ways I spent the weeks before we moved

1. Making a double-wave friendship bracelet to send to Millie at camp

2. Steering clear of Ted in general

3. Watching skateboarders do tricks by the Prospect Park Bandshell (Was skateboarding popular in Clover Gap like it was here? I had no idea.)

4. Eating ice cream from my favorite ice cream place, Happy Cone, as often as I could

5. Riding my bike to Brooklyn Heights with my dad so we could go to the Promenade and try to memorize the Manhattan skyline

6. Celebrating my birthday with spicy tuna and Alaska rolls at my favorite Japanese restaurant, Ariyoshi (I was trying to get my fill since Dad told me he didn't think there were any sushi places in our new town.)

7. To quote my mom, "moping around." She kept saying I should call one of my friends other than Millie, but there wasn't really anyone else I wanted to call. Sure, there were kids I was friendly with at school, but they all had their own things going on in the summer (day camps, trips to the beach, art classes—the same things I would have been doing if we weren't about to move). And the truth was, Millie and I had always spent so much time together that there hadn't been a lot of space for anyone else. It had never seemed like a big deal until now.

**Four things I learned when I googled Clover Gap**

------------------------------------------------------------

1. Population: 8,432 (I didn't think that sounded that small until Dad told me that the population of Brooklyn was more than 2 million, and that there were something like 50,000 people in our neighborhood alone.)

2. It prides itself on being "the Clover Capital of the Northeast." (Who knew that was a thing?)

3. Every spring it hosts Clover Fest, and people "come from far and wide to celebrate the beautiful simplicity of the clover." Interesting. I'd never thought of clovers as either beautiful or simple. I'd never really thought of them at all.

4. Notable wildlife: squirrels, chipmunks, foxes, groundhogs, deer, turkeys, raccoons, and (gulp) bears

GRRRRRR

# AUGUST

**Six things we found under the furniture the day the movers came**

-----------------------------------------------------------------

1. Two library books we thought we'd lost (mine)

2. Three loose drumsticks (Ted's)

3. A Rolling Stones record album (Even though we don't have an old-fashioned record player, Dad held on to a bunch of his old albums "for sentimental and aesthetic reasons." So he was super excited when that one turned up.)

4. A recipe for my grandma's soda bread (Mom's)

5. A funny old note from Millie, asking if I wanted to sleep over at her house and warning me that her dad snores so loud she can hear it in her room across their apartment (mine)

6. *The Pinballs,* my lost book from Mrs. Simmons's room. Mystery solved.

**Three things the men from Clover Gap Movers said when they arrived**

-------------------------------------------------------------------

1. Wow, this is such a cool neighborhood!

2. It's nothing like the boonies in Clover Gap.

3. Why would you ever want to leave the big city?

With each new question they asked, Dad looked increasingly despondent. Finally he said, "Come on, guys: Clover Gap is great too, right?" The men looked at each other for a second; then one of them turned and went to open the back of the truck. The other one shrugged and said, "It's nothing like this place."

**Eight things I threw into my backpack before getting into the car to leave Brooklyn**

-------------------------------------------------------------------

1. A pen

2. My book of lists

3. A book called *Homesick* (Mom said she read it when she was a kid and thought I might appreciate it right about now.)

4. Three granola bars

5. Peanut butter crackers

6. A drawing pad

7. Mom's old iPod (which I'm trying to get everyone to start calling "Annie's iPod")

8. The note from Millie

**Four things Ted said to me during the seven-hour trip to Clover Gap**

----------------------------------------------------------------

1. You're on my side of the seat. (He said this one about ten times.)

2. Turn down your music.

3. That's my granola bar. (It wasn't.)

4. Wake up. We're here.

This was more than he had said to me all summer.

**Eight things I noticed about Clover Gap as we drove into town**

----------------------------------------------------------------

1. Wider streets, and no cars parked on the sides

2. Way more trees than Brooklyn

3. Also more churches

4. No sidewalks

5. Sometimes we had to slow down because we were behind a tractor.

6. Bigger yards

7. Mailboxes at the ends of the driveways

8. Bigger houses

**Three thoughts I had about my new house when we pulled up in front of it**

------------------------------------------------

1. It's kind of old.

2. It's kind of pretty.

3. It's kind of purple.

**Two reasons Mom and Dad didn't tell us the house was purple**

------------------------------------------------

1. They wanted us to be surprised. (We were.)

2. They thought we might not be happy about it. (I was. Ted wasn't.)

**Four complaints Ted had about the house**

------------------------------------------------

1. The color is stupid.

2. The floors are creaky.

3. It smells weird.

4. There are too many stairs.

**Six things I remembered Ted saying about houses over my whole life so far**

------------------------------------------------------------

1. Our apartment is too small.

2. I wish we had a house.

3. All my friends have bedrooms that are bigger than mine.

4. There's no privacy here.

5. I wish we had more than one floor.

6. It's no fun using a Slinky without stairs. (He probably hadn't said that one in about five years, but still.)

When I reminded Ted about all these things, he spoke to me for the first time since we'd arrived in Clover Gap: "Annie. STOP. REMEMBERING. THINGS!"

**Four ways I tried to cheer him up**

------------------------------------------------------------

1. I pointed out the basketball hoop in the driveway.

2. I told him there was a creek in the backyard.

3. I asked whoever would listen, "Is that an apple tree?" (It wasn't.)

4. I let him choose his room first.

**Three things that make Ted's room better than mine**

1. It's bigger.

2. It's on the third floor all by itself.

3. It has a crawl space to the attic.

**Three things about my room that are still pretty cool**

1. There's a window seat.

2. There are clouds painted on the ceiling.

3. It's beside Mom and Dad's room. (I won't admit it to Ted, but I'm kind of happy to know that in this big old creaky house, my parents will be sleeping right next door.)

**Dad's favorite things about the new house**

1. Big kitchen

Dad likes to cook, so he says he's super excited about all the drawers and counter space. (In Brooklyn, any time he made a big meal, he wound up spreading out all over the place, and there would be lettuce drying on the radiator covers and roasted vegetables cooling on top of the TV cabinet.)

2. Backyard

3. Front yard

4. Basketball hoop

5. Driveway

Every time Dad comes inside he makes a proclamation about how awesome something outside is, like he's just noticed it for the first time. ("What a joy not to have to look for a parking spot!" or "I can't believe all that grass out there is ours!") I've never seen him rave about anything this way. In fact, he's raving so much that I'm starting to think he's faking it. (He doesn't know how many times I've seen him reading the *New York Times* Metro section on his phone. Or that I've noticed how whenever he starts his iPod, the first song he chooses is "The Only Living Boy in New York.") He knows I feel bad about making us leave the city, and he's trying to keep me from seeing how much he misses it. He's already homesick.

**Mom's favorite things about the new house**
- - - - - - - - - - - - - - - - - - - - - - - - - - - - - - - - - - - - - - - - - - - -
1. Like Dad, she's crazy excited about the bigger kitchen.

2. The screened-in porch ("This will be our reading spot!" she keeps saying.)

3. It has a room off the kitchen that she can use as her office. (In Brooklyn she just used a corner of the living room for her design work. Here she has her own whole space.)

**Six things Mom and Dad want to change about the house**

----------------------------------------------

1. Rip up the old funky carpet in the living room.

2. Replace all the wobbly doorknobs.

3. Fix a shattered upstairs window.

4. Repair the porch screens so mosquitoes don't take over.

5. Paint the whole inside.

6. Patch up the leaky roof.

**Ten things for a kid to do when she has just moved and knows no one but her family**

----------------------------------------------

1. Moping some more

2. Still steering clear of Ted

3. Climbing the tree in our front yard (Turns out it's a dogwood.)

4. Looking for caterpillars on the dogwood branches, and letting them crawl on my arms

5. Watching "entirely too much TV" (according to my parents)

6. Hovering around Mom, watching her design at the computer

7. Helping Mom paint my room pale blue when

she said I was "hovering her to death" (We left the clouds on the ceiling.)

8. Making Dad a "triage list" of which doorknobs were the most wobbly (Once Dad started his new job, he didn't have much time for house stuff during the week. So he gave me little home-improvement assignments like that.)

9. Dreading the first day of school

10. Wondering if this place would ever feel like home, for any of us

# SEPTEMBER

**Four sounds that woke me on the first day of school**

1. My alarm clock (which I smacked to turn off)

2. Ted's alarm clock (which he seemed to be ignoring or sleeping through)

3. A scary metallic grinding sound, like a mechanical dinosaur was eating a car

4. Mom yelling, "Turn it off! Turn it off!"

## Five favorite sounds

1. A train on train tracks

2. The ding our computer makes when I get a new email

3. A basketball bouncing on pavement

4. The subway conductor announcing our stop in Brooklyn

5. Acorns falling on our roof in Clover Gap

## Two things I saw when I went downstairs

1. Dad scooping mounds of soggy yellow stuff out of the kitchen drain

2. Mom looking super annoyed, tapping something furiously into her phone

## Mom's pet peeves

1. People saying "I could care less" when they really mean "I couldn't care less"

2. When me, Ted, or Dad forgets to take tissues out of our pockets and they wind up in the laundry

3. Shoes all over the floor when you first walk into the house

4. MY CHILD IS AN HONOR STUDENT bumper stickers on cars

## Six things they yelled at each other next

1. Mom: I'm searching plumbers.

2. Dad: We don't need a plumber. I can figure this out.

3. Mom: We've never had a garbage disposal before. You don't know anything about them.

4. Dad: What's to know?

5. Mom: Well, for one thing, apparently, you can't dump a box of packing peanuts into one!

6. Dad: They were supposed to be biodegradable!

## After a pause, four things they said in calmer voices

1. Mom: I'm calling a plumber.

2. Dad: Plumbers are expensive.

3. Mom: So are restaurants, and that's where we'll be eating if we don't have a working sink.

4. Dad (after an even longer pause): Fine. Call a plumber.

Then Mom noticed me standing there. "Oh, honey, it's your first day of school!" she said with a weak smile. "Can I get you some breakfast?"

**Three reasons I said, "It's okay. I'll just have an apple."**

1. The sight of Dad pulling gloppy mush out of the garbage disposal didn't do much for my appetite.

2. I didn't want to stick around and watch Mom and Dad do battle with the house. The excitement they'd had about this place on our first day here seemed to be wearing a little thin.

3. Seeing as how it was my first day in a new school, I wasn't very hungry anyway.

**Eight things I was dreading about the first day of school**

1. New class

2. New teacher

3. Having to talk more than I want to

4. The teacher calling me Andromeda

5. Everyone thinking my name is weird

6. Lunch

7. Lunch

8. Lunch

**One new thing that was bothering me**

1. Mom and Dad are not happy about the new house.

**Four things I'm better at than other kids**

----------------------------------------------------------------

1. Remembering weird details, as we've established

2. Knitting (thanks to Aunt Pen)

3. Typing

4. Making eggs over easy


**Four things I'm worse at than other kids**

----------------------------------------------------------------

1. Blowing bubbles

2. Diving

3. Cartwheels

4. One-handed bike riding


**Five ways my new school is different from my school in Brooklyn**

----------------------------------------------------------------

1. It's all on one floor.

2. It's newer.

3. There's no fence around it.

4. There's a big grassy field beside the playground.

5. It goes up to sixth grade (instead of fifth), so I'll have to wait one more year to be the oldest in the school.

**One way my new school is the same as my school in Brooklyn**

---

1. It smells the same. You know, like a combination of paste and construction paper and pencil shavings and bathroom cleaner? I wonder if every school in the country is required to have that smell.

**Seven questions asked by Mrs. Silva, the school guidance counselor, in our "new student" meeting**

---

1. So, you used to live in Brooklyn?

2. What brings your family to Clover Gap? (Answer: My dad got a new job. [Also, my parents say that living in a small town will allow Ted and me to have a more "free-range" childhood. That's what they've told us, but I didn't tell Mrs. Silva this part because I hate when my parents say it. It makes it sound like we're chickens. And obviously I didn't tell Mrs. Silva my theory that we actually moved because of my big mouth and my big mistake.])

3. What is your favorite subject in school? (Answer: writing)

4. What is your least favorite subject in school? (Answer: gym, unless we're playing basketball)

5. Do you have any hobbies? (Answer: stamp

collecting. [But not really. I hate when people ask me what my hobbies are because I feel like I'm going to let them down or confuse them by saying "making lists." So I usually say the first thing that pops into my head when I hear the word "hobby," and that is "stamp collecting." I think I have three stamps.])

6. Do you have any special talents? (Answer: I'm a good writer.)

What I didn't say: Is having a crazy memory for random information considered a talent? What about blending in so well that people forget you're there? Is that a talent? If so, then those are mine. I guess those skills could make me a good spy someday. But right now I don't want to be a spy. Which brings me to Mrs. Silva's next question . . .

7. What is something you want this year? (Answer: I'd like to be faster at solving math problems.)

**Three things I didn't tell Mrs. Silva that I really want this year**

------------------------------------------------------------

1. To be a regular kid who blends in and doesn't notice or remember too much, or say the wrong things

2. For my family to be happy in Clover Gap so they'll stop caring that I made us leave Brooklyn

3. At least two new friends in my new school (I'll never meet anyone as great as Millie, but I feel like I need to try for safety in numbers. Backup friends seem like a good idea in case something goes wrong.)

I know there's a challenge here. How am I supposed to make new friends if I'm also invisible? But I don't want to get myself—or anyone else—in trouble, the way I did in Brooklyn.

**Ways to be a regular kid, blend in, and make new friends all at the same time**

1.

Okay, so I have no idea. If I could think of even one thing to put on this list, I probably would have done it in Brooklyn . . . and I wouldn't have been so nervous for the first day of school here.

**Three things that could have gone better on the first day**

1. My teacher, Mr. Allbright, could have introduced me as Annie, instead of saying Andromeda.

2. Everyone could have stayed quiet, instead of saying, "Huh? What'd he say? *What's* her name?"

3. When I spoke up to say, "Just call me Annie," my

voice could have been louder instead of coming out in a whisper.

**If I got to pick my own name, I would choose . . .**

1. Mia

2. Lulu

3. Vanessa

4. Honeybee

**Four things that could have gone worse on the first day**

1. Mr. Allbright could have made us choose our own desks. But he gave us assigned seats (so I didn't have to worry about someone telling me they were saving a seat for somebody else).

2. Mr. Allbright could have insisted on calling me Andromeda like some grown-ups do. But he listened when I whispered that he should call me Annie.

3. Mom could have put an embarrassing mushy note in my backpack the way she sometimes did when I was younger. But instead she just slipped in a little Reese's cup, with a tiny smiley face drawn on the wrapper.

4. I could have sat all alone at lunch. But I met Zora.

-------------------------------------------------------------------

1. She writes funny notes, like the one she passed
   me across the aisle in class this morning: "Did
   the teacher say his name is Mr. Allbright or Mr.
   Allright?"

After I read it, I looked around a little nervously.
(Passing a note about the teacher on the first day of
school is a pretty gutsy move.) I quickly drew a lightbulb
and wrote, "Allbright, all right?" then passed it back to
her.

2. She thinks I'm funny too. (She giggled after she
   read my answer.)

3. She's smart. Mr. Allbright made us get into pairs
   to brainstorm suggestions for classroom rules,
   and she had some good ideas (like raising our
   hands with different signs to mean different
   things—one finger up for "I have something to
   say," two fingers up for "I have a question," etc.).

4. She didn't try to make me talk too much. When I told her I didn't want to tell our rules to the class, she said, "That's okay. You can be the note taker."

5. She isn't shy. When I walked into the lunchroom, she saw me looking around for a seat, and she waved her arms like crazy and yelled, "Annie! Come sit over here!"

6. She is a pescatarian. That means the only kind of animal she'll eat is fish.

7. She has a cat with no tail. No one knows how it got that way.

8. She has an older brother who's in the same grade as Ted and a younger brother who's six.

9. Her mom grew up in Clover Gap.

10. Her dad is from Jamaica.

11. She goes to Jamaica during every winter and summer break to visit her grandparents, who still live there.


**Three other kids at Zora's lunch table**

--------------------------------------------------------------------

1. Charlie (likes to draw Star Wars characters, was wearing a fedora and sunglasses before school this morning)

2. Zachary (talks about Legos *a lot*)

3. Amelia (laughs at everything Zora says, carries a heart-shaped lunch box)

**Four things Amelia did that made me feel weird**

1. Changed the subject when Zora introduced me.

2. Looked at everyone but me every time she talked.

3. Rolled her eyes when I said I thought Mr. Allbright seemed nice.

4. Offered cookies to the other kids, then looked at me and said, "Sorry, I don't have enough. I didn't know there'd be another person at our table."

**Four more not-so-great things about the first day**

1. I made a wrong turn on my way to the bathroom and a third grader had to point me in the right direction.

2. Three more people called me Andromeda (the PE teacher, the school secretary, and the nurse when I dropped off a medical form my parents forgot).

3. I didn't know there was an afternoon snack time, so I hadn't brought anything to eat after lunch.

4. I kept thinking about Millie and wondering what she was doing in Brooklyn.

**Three more sort-of-good things about the first day**

1. Zora shared her snack (pretzels and hummus) with me.

2. Our classroom has a lizard named Harvey.

3. I only got lost the one time.

**Nine questions Mom had to ask me before I told her all the details of my day**

1. How was school?

2. Do you like your teacher?

3. How were the other kids?

4. Did it seem really different from Brooklyn?

5. What are your classmates like?

6. Who did you sit with at lunch?

7. What did you talk about at lunch?

8. Were those kids all friends already?

9. So all the kids were nice?

Finally I told her: All the kids were mostly nice. But one kid, Amelia, was kind of snotty. I told her about the cookies.

**Mom's sympathetic list of times people were mean to her**

1. When she was six, a big kid at the pool pushed her into the deep end and she freaked out because she wasn't a good swimmer. The lifeguard fished her out and yelled at her for being in the deep end when she hadn't taken a swim test.

2. When she was nine, some girls in her class wouldn't let her be in their secret club.

3. When she was ten, she had to borrow her mother's sunglasses on Hats and Shades Day at school (because she didn't have her own), and a girl in her grade made fun of her because they were so uncool.

4. When she was thirteen, a boy told her he wouldn't dance with her at a school dance because she was too tall.

After hearing this list, I felt a little better about Amelia. But I also felt pretty sad for Mom.

**One thing Ted told Mom about his first day of school (before going to his room and blasting his music)**

1. It's different.

**Three things I told Millie in my email to her that afternoon**

---

1. My teacher's name

2. The names of the kids I sat with

3. That I thought the new kids were nice, but I could tell they weren't going to be as fun as she was

I didn't know if that last part was true—it was really too soon to know how fun anyone was going to be. But I didn't want Millie to think I was in danger of making a new best friend.

**Seven ways my new town is different from my old one**

---

1. People drive almost everywhere.

2. There is no train here.

3. There is no city nearby.

4. I was right—there are more bugs. Like spiders in our basement. And I heard someone say something about snakes, so I'm watching out for those, too. No bears so far.

5. I take the bus home from school instead of walking.

6. Most people here are white, and it seems like there are way fewer people with other skin colors. Or people from other countries. Or with different religions. ("Yes, it's pretty homogeneous," my mom sighed when I told her that Zora and her brothers were some of the only black kids at school.)

7. There are different rules.

**Three rules in my new town that I didn't have in my old town**

-----------------------------------------------------------------

1. Call all grown-ups Mr. or Mrs., even if they aren't teachers.

2. Dogs do not have to be on leashes. (I guess this is the opposite of a rule; it's like an un-rule. They just wander around the neighborhood as they please.)

3. Take off your hat when you're inside. (This is a tough one for Ted, who loves his Brooklyn Cyclones baseball cap.)

**Three ways Ted drives me nuts every day after school**

---------------------------------------------------------------

1. The drumming. Seriously. (His bedroom is right above mine, and the racket is constant.)

2. Hogging the basketball hoop while he practices his free throw

3. Burping the alphabet


**Two reasons Mom says I should be patient with Ted**

---------------------------------------------------------------

1. He's at a "difficult age."

2. He had a bunch of friends back in Brooklyn, and he hasn't really "connected with anyone here yet." (I feel like saying, "I had friends in Brooklyn too!" I mean, mostly Millie, but still, it's not like moving was easy for me. Even if it was my fault. *Especially* if it was my fault.)


**Four ways Mom and Dad are trying to keep Ted occupied**

---------------------------------------------------------------

1. Taking us to free concerts at the Clover Gapitheater, which Ted always complains are "just a bunch of old guys playing banjos and tubas"

2. Drum lessons with a man named Mr. Tapper (That was actually their gift to Ted for his birthday this year, not long after we moved. I think they hoped it would be a good way for Ted to meet

people, but it turns out he's the only one in the class. Dad keeps saying what a brilliant name Tapper is for a drum teacher; Ted keeps saying he is just another old guy who doesn't let him "riff" enough.)

3. Making him do yard work (Ted has pointed out that some kids get paid to mow lawns and trim bushes. Dad's response: "And aren't we lucky that we have you to do it for nothing?")

4. Making him fold laundry. He is not exactly an expert at this. (I know he's been on folding duty when I find socks and underwear inside my shirtsleeves and pant legs the next day.)

## My three least-favorite parts of school

1. Turn-and-talk time during morning meeting (see earlier: "Four reasons I'm quiet")

2. Oral presentations

3. Kickball

We never really played kickball in Brooklyn. Kids there played wall ball or four square, and if I had a choice, I would usually hang with Millie and draw with sidewalk chalk instead. But the truth is, even if I had gone to some kind of serious kickball academy my whole life, I'm pretty sure I would still be terrible at this game.

**Five everyday objects that freak me out**

-------------------------------------------------

1. Porcelain dolls

2. Toy clowns

3. Can openers

4. Brillo pads

5. Kickballs

**Eight things that happen during an average kickball game at my new school**

-------------------------------------------------

1. When one of the power kickers (like Charlie or Scarlett) goes up to kick, star pitcher Barry Seigler yells, "Back up!"

2. All the kids in the outfield back up like fifty feet, to the edge of the playground. This is because the power kickers have mighty kicks that can send the ball into orbit.

3. After the ball goes into orbit, everyone on that team cheers.

4. When it's my turn to kick, Barry yells, "It's Annie." (I will admit this is an improvement over "It's the new kid!" which is what he said for the first couple of days of school.)

5. The outfield kids all run forward and make a semicircle about ten feet away from me. (Because I do *not* have a mighty kick.)

6. I kick, the ball goes about three feet, and someone immediately catches it and tags me out.

7. No one on my team cheers, of course. (The kids on the other team cheer a little.)

8. I return to the bench and sit with the one other person in the class who appears to have no interest in kickball, a girl named Kate.

**Two other things I have noticed during kickball games**

1. Charlie cheers especially enthusiastically for Zora. He cheers so much that I'm starting to wonder if he has a crush on her.

2. Kate is always humming on the bench.

**Four things about Kate**

1. Hums a lot

2. Wears glasses

3. Doesn't seem to care what she does at lunch (sometimes sits with Zora and Amelia and me, sometimes sits with Scarlett and her twin sister, Josie, sometimes helps Mrs. Otis, the librarian, shelve books)

4. Reads a book on the school bus, and doesn't care where she sits there, either

**Two of the most embarrassing moments in my life (before today's kickball game)**

1. When my kindergarten teacher, Miss Bell, saw me sucking my thumb in the backseat of my car after school

2. The time I hugged a stranger's legs in line at the post office because I mistakenly thought he was my dad

**My one most embarrassing moment (after today's kickball game)**

1. Underwear flying out of the leg of my jeans after a kick

**Twelve events leading up to the airborne-underwear incident**

1. My jeans felt uncomfortable all morning, especially on the left leg. I mentioned it to Mom and she said that I was probably just outgrowing them, but there was no time to change if I was going to catch the bus.

2. As usual, we played kickball that afternoon.

3. When my turn came to kick, the outfield crew ran up to greet me like they always did.

4. I ran toward the ball, and for once I actually gave it a respectable kick!

5. It flew up, up, up into the air . . . and so did something else.

6. Just when I should have been pumped about my best kick ever, I was horrified to discover that the reason my jeans had felt weird all day was that something was stuck inside them. It was a pair of polka-dotted underwear, left jammed inside my jeans leg by the world's worst laundry folder, my brother, Ted. But the underwear was not stuck anymore! No, it was soaring into the air . . . straight into the waiting hands of star pitcher Barry Seigler.

7. Barry started yelling, "Underwear! Ew, it's underwear! *Girls'* underwear!"

8. Although it seemed beside the point to tell him that the underwear was clean, I tried anyway. "Oh, sorry; those must have been crumpled in my jeans. They're not dirty," I said.

9. Barry threw the underwear onto the ground and started yelling for hand sanitizer.

10. Everyone else was doubled over laughing.

11. Everyone, that is, except for the super-focused Angela Havens, who grabbed the ball, ran with it to first base, and got me out.

12. I retrieved my underwear, slunk back to my place on the bench beside the humming Kate, and made a mental note to strangle my brother.

**Two people who tried to cheer me up after the flying-underwear fiasco**

1. Kate (She said Barry was always doing gross things like picking his nose and wiping it under his desk, so she thought he deserved to get attacked by my underwear.)

2. Zora (After the game she came up to me, put her arm around my shoulders, and said, "Annie, you might have invented a new game: capture the dirty laundry!" When I insisted that it was clean laundry, she said, "I know, I know. I'm just glad someone grossed *Barry* out for a change.")

**One person who apparently is never going to forget the flying-underwear fiasco**

---

1. Amelia, who laughed so hard she cried and actually said, "I am never going to forget this!"


**One person who finally made me feel a little better about the whole mortifying situation**

---

1. Millie


When I got home, instead of heading straight to the pantry for a snack, I told Mom I had to call Millie.


**Three things Millie said that made me laugh after I told her the underwear story**

---

1. You should just tell them that's how we play it in Brooklyn. Call it undie-ball.

2. You should hide all Ted's underwear next time he's in the shower.

3. That still isn't as bad as the time I peed in my leotard onstage when I was a snowflake in the *Nutcracker.*


She's right; it wasn't. And even though she cheered me up, our conversation made me miss her even more. And I was still livid at Ted.

**Two things I said to Ted when he got home**

1. You messed up the laundry!

2. Underwear flew out of my jeans leg in kickball and it was your stupid fault!

**Two things Ted said back to me**

1. That is the funniest thing I ever heard.

2. Fold your own dumb laundry if you don't like the way I do it.

**Eight downward spirals the conversation took from there**

1. I accused Ted of being a giant drag who was always grumping around the house because he had no friends.

2. Ted told me it was my fault we had to move to this stupid town where he had no friends, and where he wouldn't be able to go to high school for music.

3. I told him he wasn't even that good at drumming, and that he would make friends here if he wasn't so lame.

4. He told me Zora was only my friend because she felt sorry for me.

5. Mom heard us yelling and told us to separate from each other.

6. Ted yelled, "I am not folding her laundry anymore!"

7. Mom said, "Fair enough."

8. Ted went outside to shoot baskets, slamming the front door on his way.

So I seized my chance to explore an off-limits place: the attic crawl space off Ted's room.

### Things I suspected were in Ted's attic crawl space

1. Stuff he never lets me touch, like his iPad and the bongos he bought at a street fair in our old neighborhood

2. Old CDs Uncle Dan gave him (the ones Mom said had inappropriate lyrics)

3. Money

### Three things that were actually in Ted's attic crawl space

1. Spiders

2. His stuffed dinosaur, Jerome, which I thought he'd given away

3. A box of old papers Mom and Dad had stored there

### Three boring things in the box of old papers

1. Tax forms (yawn)

2. Bills (snooze)

3. A folder labeled TRANSCRIPTS/RÉSUMÉS (snoreburger)

### Two cute things in the box of old papers

1. Ted's and my old school pictures

2. Ted's and my preschool artwork

### One confusing thing in the box of old papers

1. A letter from Dad's old company in Brooklyn, addressed to Dad, with the words "Severance Agreement" at the top

**Two things the word "severance" makes me think of**

------------------------------------------------------------

1. Cutting off a toe or finger

2. Harry Potter's Potions teacher

I'm pretty sure this letter has nothing to do with either of those, but it still doesn't sound good. I would ask Ted if he knows what it means, but we aren't speaking to each other. Also, I don't want him to know I was in "his" attic. But I know I'll remember that letter.

**My nine favorite words, just because**

------------------------------------------------------------

1. Morbid

2. Lantern

3. Flurry

4. Hen

5. Croon

6. Hammock

7. Woolen

8. Storm

9. Wretched

## My six least favorite words

--------------------------------------------------------------------

1. Toilet

2. Chore

3. Random

4. Grizzly

5. Clammy

6. Delectable

# OCTOBER

Five challenges for a new kid in school (besides the obvious ones like finding a seat at lunch and making friends)

---------------------------------------------------------------

1. Don't get lost when you have to see the school nurse or deliver something to another teacher. (So far, I'm not doing so great on this one; apparently, I have a terrible sense of direction.)

2. Figure out who's who. (There are two kids in the class next to mine named Molly and Maggie. For all of September I thought Molly was Maggie, and vice versa. Frustrating for someone who's used to knowing who everyone is.)

3. Try not to look too awkward when other kids get super excited and greet "celebrity" teachers they all know well. (My old school had these too—the favorite kindergarten teacher, the fun PE teacher, the cool art teacher, etc.)

4. Don't break the unspoken rules for school events like Pajama Day (wear a T-shirt and flannel pants, *not* a nightgown; luckily, I was on target with that one) and Fall Festival (the bounce house is for the little kids; fifth graders head for the corn maze).

5. Find something to do on weekends.

On weekends in Brooklyn, I'd either go to a museum or a concert with my family, eat dinner with my parents' friends and their kids, picnic in the park, or have a sleepover with Millie. Sometimes all those things. But we're still figuring it out here. I've heard other kids talking about sleepovers, but I know I'm not close enough to anyone here yet to invite them over. And no one has invited me, either. So there's been a lot of family togetherness on weekends.

**My parents' top five things to do on fall weekends in Clover Gap**

-------------------------------------------------------------------

1. Shop for "antiques." (Even though our new house isn't huge, it's still a lot bigger than our apartment was. Which means we now have a lot of space with no furniture in it. But new furniture is expensive, so we go to stores that sell old stuff. Mom says they're antiques; Dad calls it junk. Either way, they almost never find anything that's "in their price range," which I know is their way of saying that even old stuff is still too expensive

for us.) Come to think of it, maybe these shopping trips are only one of Mom's favorite things to do. Because Dad is usually really quiet by the end of them, and when we get home he goes straight to his iPod and his big noise-canceling headphones for a while.

2. Go "leaf-peeping." (I don't know why this is what it's called when you just drive around and look at the leaf colors in fall. It's not like you're sneaking up on the leaves or trying to get a secret glimpse of them. I pointed this out to Mom on one of our drives, and she said she thinks people just like to make up rhyming names for things. Then I told her "leaf-peeping" doesn't exactly rhyme, and she sighed and said, "You got me, Annie. It's a mystery." It was obvious she didn't want to talk about it. My parents don't really want to talk about much of anything on our leaf-peeping trips. Mom says it's "meditative" to drive around quietly and look at trees. I wonder if she's meditating about how hard life has been since I made us move. But I don't ask that question.)

3. Rake leaves.

4. Make Ted and me rake leaves when they get tired.

5. Repeatedly sniff the air and say, "It just smells like fall!"

## Ted's favorite thing to do on fall weekends in Clover Gap
----------------------------------------------------------------

1. Go for long bike rides that always seem to start right when Mom and Dad are about to tell us to rake leaves.

## One thing Ted missed while he was on a long bike ride
----------------------------------------------------------------

1. Dad almost falling off the roof

## Two things that nearly drove Dad over the edge, literally
----------------------------------------------------------------

1. He was checking out a spot on the roof above Ted's room where he thought there might be water damage. (Mom wanted to call a roofer, but Dad insisted on investigating it himself.)

2. As he was climbing to the top, he lost his footing and slid to the very edge of the roof. He dug in his heels and stopped just before he would have gone over (but not before kicking a gutter and knocking it loose, sending a shower of smelly wet leaves cascading onto the front steps).

## One conversation that followed

1. Mom: THAT'S IT! I'm calling a roofer.

2. Dad (trying to save face with a chuckle): Phew, okay! I guess that's Dad, zero; house, one.

I decided not to point out that the house's score should actually be much higher, if you count the clogged garbage disposal, the window that slammed onto his hand last week, and the bathroom mirror he accidentally ripped off the wall because he thought it was the door to a medicine cabinet. Poor Dad.

## My favorite thing about fall in Clover Gap

1. So far, the leaves. I have to admit they're pretty amazing. City trees never turned colors the way these do. The raking is a drag, but once in a while I find a leaf that's so perfect I have to save it and press it in the pages of our giant old dictionary.

## Favorite pastime for the rest of Clover Gap in fall

1. Football (specifically, rooting for the football team at Clover Gap High on Friday nights)

## Number of football games I had been to before moving to Clover Gap

1. Zero

Football just wasn't a big deal in Brooklyn. I mean, sometimes my dad would watch it on TV on Sundays, but it's not like he was a superfan. And I never cared about it at all. ("Superfan" is a word I learned recently. Lots of the people here in Clover Gap are superfans.)

**Number of football games most people in Clover Gap go to in a year**

1. Five, if you are just a fan and you are going only to the home games

2. Twelve, if you are a superfan and you go to ALL the games

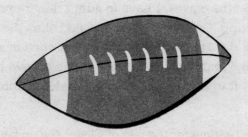

It seems that most of my friends' families are just fans, with the exception of Charlie's family. His parents belong to the booster club and take Charlie and his brother to all the away games. Charlie says if he doesn't make the team when we're in high school, his dad told him there'll be "hell to pay." Yowza.

**One person who refused to join in when my parents said we should check out a game**

1. Ted

He said football is boring and he had to do homework anyway. (I think Mom and Dad suspect that he doesn't want to have to hang out with his parents at a place where all the other kids his age will be with their friends. At least I *think* that's what they're thinking. They didn't push him, but they gave each other a look that I didn't really understand.)

**Five ways my parents and I looked out of place at our first Clover Gap High football game**

1. We were wearing regular clothes instead of team sweatshirts.

2. We didn't have green-and-white pompoms.

3. We didn't have giant green foam fingers.

4. We didn't know the team cheers.

5. We weren't chatting with people all around us. (In fact, we weren't chatting with anyone at all, because we didn't know anybody.)

**Three people who saved the day**

1. Zora

2. Zora's mom (wearing a CGHS ALUMNI jacket)

3. Zora's dad (guiding Zora's little brother, Jackson, up the bleacher steps and telling him not to bop anyone with his foam finger)

## Five ways Zora's family rescued us

1. They sat with us (after Zora spied me in the bleachers, waved like crazy, and steered her parents to our spot).

2. They introduced us to the people in front of us, behind us, and on either side of us. (I could see where Zora got her personality from; no one in her family is shy.)

3. Zora's mom gave Mom and me their extra pompoms so we would look a little more spirited.

4. Zora's dad gave my dad a program so he would know who the players were. (He said he got the program for Zora's older brother, Marcus, but since Marcus was wandering around with his friends somewhere, Dad could keep it.)

5. Zora's mom told us we should stay in our seats during halftime because the marching band was as good as the football team. (She was right; the band was my favorite part.)

**Six things Mom said on the way home from the game (Clover Gap won, by the way)**

------------------------------------------------------------

1. Wasn't that fun?

2. Thank goodness Zora saw you.

3. Her family is so nice.

4. Isn't her older brother Ted's age?

5. Maybe we can convince Ted to come next time.

6. I feel like we learned a lot about the town tonight.

She sounded more than just happy; she sounded relieved. It occurred to me that my parents have to navigate "new kid" challenges sometimes too.

For me, the next new-kid thing to figure out was around the corner: Halloween.

**One more rule in Clover Gap that we didn't have in Brooklyn**

------------------------------------------------------------

1. For Halloween, you can't dress up as anything too scary.

**Five Halloween costumes I was considering**

------------------------------------------------------------

1. Angry cheerleader

2. Mad scientist

3. Witch doctor

4. Rotting pumpkin

5. Evil fairy

I asked Zora if she thought these would pass the "not too scary" test at school, and she said yes, that as long as nothing involved blood or weapons, I should be okay. She voted for evil fairy. Since I already had the wings from when I was a regular fairy in first grade, I went with that one. (Besides, Halloween was two days away and Mom told me there was no way she was making a whole new costume before then. And I knew that buying something was out of the question—anytime Ted asks for something new these days, Mom reminds him that "moving was expensive and we're still trying to save money." I never ask. Mom always says she appreciates how "unmaterialistic" I am. I think I'm just more sensitive than Ted when it comes to asking for unnecessary stuff. And I know I notice more, like the way Mom has gone a long time without getting her hair cut, and the fact that she and Dad empty out their coin jar more often than they used to. It's not hard—for me, at least—to see that it's not such a good idea to ask for too much.)

### One opinion Zora had about evil fairies

1. They should have cramazing hair. (She said "cramazing" was a combination of "crazy" and "amazing.")

### My new most embarrassing moment after today

1. Walking in the Halloween parade with a hairbrush stuck in my hair

### Fifteen events leading up to my shame parade

1. When Mr. Allbright said we could close our math workbooks and start getting ready for the parade, I told Zora I wasn't sure what she had in mind for my cramazing fairy hair.

2. She said she would show me.

3. Zora hovered over me, winding sections of my hair around the spiky crown of dyed-black pinecones Mom had made me to top off my evil look.

4. Zora had to leave to go to the bathroom and fix the whiskers on her cat costume.

5. I told her I could finish my hair. The only spot that wasn't done was in the front, right above my forehead.

6. I tried looping hair around the crown the way I thought Zora had, but it didn't look quite right.

7. I tucked the brush under the crown and tried to pull a chunk of hair through with it.

8. The brush stopped. It wouldn't budge. Neither would the crown. Neither would my hair.

9. Zora returned from the bathroom.

10. Mr. Allbright told us we had to line up for the parade.

11. I told him the hairbrush was stuck.

12. He briefly tried to untangle it and was unsuccessful. So was Zora.

13. He suggested that I tell people I was "a hair fairy."

14. I asked if I could stay in the classroom during the parade.

15. He said no.

**Two responses the kids from other classes had when they saw me in the parade**

1. What's the new kid supposed to be?

2. Hey, there's a brush stuck in your hair! (No kidding.)

**One thing Zora chanted as she marched in front of me**

1. She's an evil hair fairy! You better watch out!

I had to smile then. Zora is a pretty good friend to have, even if it was her idea to give me cramazing hair.

**Five ways Halloween got better after that**

1. Zora asked if I wanted to go home with her after school so she could fix my hair.

2. She also asked if I wanted to go trick-or-treating together later.

3. She told me Amelia was trick-or-treating in her own neighborhood with her older cousin. (I was pretty glad Amelia wouldn't be around to make private jokes with Zora or remind everyone about my flying underwear.)

4. I got to see Zora's house for the first time.

5. Mom said Zora could come to our house after trick-or-treating.

**Four cool things about Zora's house**

1. There's a tire swing hanging from the highest branch of an oak tree in the backyard.

2. Her mom makes amazing oatmeal cookies.

3. Zora and her brothers have pictures taped up all over their bedroom walls. Some of them are cut from magazines, but most are ones they drew themselves. (Zora's pictures are all cats; her older brother draws a lot of guitars. And her younger brother's are mostly his name above stick-figure self-portraits.)

4. There were elaborate blanket forts set up in two different rooms. They were built by Zora's older brother, Marcus, for her younger brother, Jackson.

**Three things Zora said while we ate oatmeal cookies in her room**

1. Are you over the underwear incident yet? (Me: Almost.)

2. Don't worry; everyone else has moved on from that.

3. Now they're talking about other things. Like crushes.

**Three examples of crushes Zora knew of**

1. Angela has a crush on Derek.

2. Xavier has a crush on Keira.

3. Raymond has a crush on Olivia.

**One crush *I* knew of that was not news to Zora**

1. "I think Charlie might have a crush on you."

**Three ways I would react if I heard someone had a crush on me**

1. Blush

2. Get a rumbly stomach

3. Ask for evidence of the crush

**Two ways Zora reacted when I mentioned the Charlie crush**

1. Ha, I know. Everyone says that.

2. He's just my friend. But it doesn't matter anyway because his grandmother would flip out if she knew he liked me.

Charlie's grandmother lives with his family and takes care of him after school. She's at pickup and other school stuff more than any other grandparents are; she has short black hair that's sprayed into place, and she is always smiling in this way that looks forced (kind of like the smile is held on by hairspray too).

**One answer Zora gave when I asked why Charlie's grandmother would care if he liked her**

---

1. Because I'm black.

**Two questions I asked after Zora told me that**

---

1. Are you serious?! (I have to admit I was shocked. In Brooklyn, lots of kids I knew had parents of different races. Besides, we're in fifth grade; it's not like having a crush on someone means you're going to marry her. But Zora didn't even seem surprised.)

2. How do you know that? (Zora's answer: My mom has known their family for a long time. She and Charlie's mom were in the same class in third grade, and there was only one other black kid in the class, Carl. When Charlie's mom had a birthday party at her pool, the whole class was invited . . . except for Mom and Carl. My grandma called Charlie's grandma to ask what was up, and all she said was "It's a pool party. I'm sure you understand.")

## Four responses I had to this story

1. I don't get it. (Zora said she didn't either at first. But then her mom told her that was a thing back then, that some white people thought it was bad to share a swimming pool with people of other skin colors.)

2. I don't get that, either. (Zora: Me neither.)

3. That's really awful. Your poor mom. (Zora: Yeah, it's a pretty bad memory for her. She was really upset. My grandparents took her to the circus that weekend instead, to try to take her mind off it, and now she says the circus always reminds her of that birthday party, but it also reminds her of how much her parents loved her.)

4. Maybe Charlie's grandma isn't like that anymore. (Zora: I'm pretty sure she is. She's always icy when I see her. And, whatever . . . maybe it will make Charlie keep his crushy feelings to himself.)

But I wondered if Zora really thought "whatever" about Charlie's grandma. The story about her mom and the birthday party was one of the saddest things I'd ever heard. (It made my mom's old mean-kid stories seem like no big deal.)

**Three interruptions to my train of thought about Zora's mom**

-----------------------------------------------------------------

1. Zora's dad popped his head in and said, "Hey, Z. Do you know what time it is?"

2. Zora looked at her clock, jumped up, and said, "We have to trick-or-treat!"

3. Then she said, "Dad, you said I could just go with my friends this year, right? No parents?"

Her dad sighed and said, "Yes, I guess I promised." I called my parents and they said it was okay too.

**Four Halloween firsts I had that night**

-----------------------------------------------------------------

1. Trick-or-treating without one of my parents

2. Trick-or-treating at houses instead of stores or apartments like we did in the city

3. Trick-or-treating with boys who weren't Ted and his friends (We saw Zach and Charlie at the third house we went to, and they stayed with us the rest of the way.)

4. First real haunted house

**How this haunted house was different from others I'd been to**
--------------------------------------------------------------------

1. It was not sponsored by the PTA.

2. It did not feature spaghetti being presented as worms and peeled grapes masquerading as eyeballs.

3. There were no high school kids in rubber masks answering the door.

4. It was, according to Zora, Charlie, and Zach, *an actual haunted house*.


**Five reasons they say the house is haunted**
--------------------------------------------------------------------

1. It has been boarded up for as long as they can remember, but sometimes the front door is mysteriously open.

2. No one has ever been seen coming out of the house.

3. Years ago, a college student collecting signatures for a clean-water bill entered the open front door, and she was never seen again.

4. The attic window is the only one not boarded up, and if you look closely, sometimes you can see a pale white figure moving in front of it.

5. If you knock on the door on Halloween night, you will hear terrible shrieks coming from inside. And every neighborhood kid is supposed to try it the first time he or she goes trick-or-treating without parents. That meant us. Right then.

**Five things that crossed my mind to say at that moment**

1. That sounds terrifying.

2. That's trespassing.

3. I don't think my mom would like this idea.

4. Zach isn't a very fast runner. That could be a problem if we need a quick getaway. (I knew this because he and I were in the same group the day the gym teacher timed us in the fifty-yard dash. I'm not faster than many people, but I was faster than Zach.)

5. Don't you guys just want to go get some candy?

**One thing I did say at that moment**

1. Um, you mean now?

But I still followed them. Turns out my fear of not making friends is stronger than my fear of haunted houses.

**Seven things we heard at the haunted house**

1. The creak of the iron gate in front of the house as we opened it

2. Our own breathing as we walked slowly down the path from the gate to the house

3. More creaking as we moved gingerly onto the rotting porch steps

4. Someone's dad on the sidewalk yelling, "Hey! What are you kids doing over there?"

5. A crash as Zach turned around, stepped on a rotten spot, and put his foot through one of the porch floorboards

6. Charlie yelling, "Run for it!"

7. The sound of Charlie running as Zora and I helped Zach pull his foot out of the porch floor

**One thing we did not hear at the haunted house**

1. Terrible shrieks (other than the ones coming from Zach)

**Four reasons we only went trick-or-treating at five more houses after that**

1. Zach stopped to yell at Charlie for abandoning him on the porch.

2. Charlie was defensive and insisted he ran because he saw a ghostly figure through the window.

3. Zach was limping.

4. Zach was bleeding a little. Finally I said we were near my house and we could go there to get him a bandage and check out his ankle.

**Five best things in my Halloween haul**

1. Reese's pumpkins

2. Butterfingers

3. Nerds

4. M&M's

5. Plastic witch nose

**Five worst things in my Halloween haul**

------------------------------------------------------------------

1. Pencils

2. Granola bar

3. Apple

4. Black licorice

5. Candy corn

I know, I know, some people love candy corn. I am not one of those people. And neither is Zora. But my mom is, so I told Zora we could give it to her when we got back to my house.

**Five things you would notice about my family if you spent an hour with them**

------------------------------------------------------------------

1. My mom has a little bit of an accent. She grew up in North Carolina, and sometimes she'll say things like "y'all" or "I reckon." (She doesn't mind the rule about calling grown-ups Mr. and Mrs. here. She says that's what she had to do when she was a kid.)

2. Mom is really smart, but kind of forgetful. She is like me, actually. She remembers things about people she hasn't seen in decades, but she forgets to put the chicken in the fridge when she gets home from the grocery store. And when she's

working, she gets focused on her designs (and it can be hard to get her attention).

3. My dad is really into Harry Potter. Sometimes I think it's funny, but sometimes it's a little weird.

4. Dad also loves music. LOVES it. He has to turn it on as soon as he walks in the house or gets in the car, and sometimes Mom gets annoyed. (She likes music too, but she can't have it on all the time, especially if she's working. She says it "crowds her thinking space." It hasn't been much of a problem since we moved, because Dad usually uses his headphones these days. I guess he doesn't feel like sharing his tunes as much as he used to.)

5. Besides the drumming, I'm not sure what you'd notice about Ted. Ever since we moved, he keeps to himself a lot. He didn't even dress up for Halloween, and it used to be his favorite holiday. In Brooklyn, he and his friends would always dress up as a group of things that went together, like the members of Nirvana or all the Batman villains or something like that. This year, he just came home and went to his room like always.

**Three good things that happened back at my house**

1. Turned out Zach only needed a Band-Aid and an ice pack.

2. Charlie gave me his Reese's pumpkins because he's allergic to peanuts.

3. Mom didn't ask anyone too many questions.

### Four things that embarrassed me back at my house

1. When Dad saw how much candy we got, he said, "Merlin's beard!," his favorite Harry Potter expression.

2. Mom was singing along really loudly to her Johnny Cash CD when we walked in.

3. The carpet in the living room was partially ripped away, and you could see the gross plywood floor underneath. (Mom and Dad were disappointed when they started tearing up the carpet and didn't find nice hardwood under it. Now we're "in a holding pattern" while they figure out what to do.)

4. Zora asked if anyone remembered who gave us the granola bars, and Dad said, "I'm sure Annie does! She has an amazing memory." (I did remember. It was Mrs. Deibler. She lives one block over in a yellow house, and she has four-year-old twin boys named Ethan and Andrew. She was wearing a black skirt, a red sweater, and fuzzy slippers, and when she gave us the granola bars, she said, "Something crunchy for Halloween!" But I said I didn't remember. And Zora gave me a funny look.)

### One thing Ted said to me after my friends left

1. You totally remembered who gave you the granola bars, didn't you?

### Two things I wanted to say back to Ted

1. Yes, I remembered.

2. Do you know what a severance agreement is? And why Dad got one?

### One thing I actually said to Ted

1. Why were you spying on us, weirdo? I'm going to bed.

But first I had to check my email. Halloween was always the best day in Brooklyn, and I wanted to see if I had a report from Millie.

### Four ways Millie's Halloween sounded awesome

1. The city closed off the street for three extra blocks for the neighborhood parade this year. (I knew the neighborhood Halloween parade was going to be one of the things I missed most. It's not like a regular parade where people stand on the side and watch while floats and bands go by. There's some of that stuff at the beginning, but mostly everyone just walks in the street with hundreds of

other people, checking out each other's costumes, saying hi to people they know, and trading candy.)

2. There were people dressed as fire-breathing dragons on stilts in the parade.

3. She and two other kids dressed up as a fork, a knife, and a spoon. (What two other kids, I wondered. That seemed like an important detail to leave out.)

4. Her parents let her stay at the parade till ten-thirty.

**Three ways I told her my Halloween was awesome**

1. I was an evil fairy.

2. I got to go trick-or-treating with just friends, no parents.

3. I went to a real haunted house.

I didn't tell her that we didn't actually go inside the haunted house. So I guess Millie wasn't the only one omitting details.

# NOVEMBER

**Three weird smells in our new house**

------------------------------------------------------------

1. Wood smoke (This one lingered for a while after Dad forgot to open the chimney flue the first time he built a fire in the fireplace.)

2. Paint (Mom and Dad are painting the rooms at an average of about one a month. The latest was the dining room, which they want to have ready in time for Thanksgiving.)

3. Something mysterious and fierce that we eventually determined was half of an old turkey sandwich in the bottom of Ted's backpack

**Five things that fell out of Ted's backpack when he dumped it upside down to clean it**

------------------------------------------------------------

1. Two books (*Catcher in the Rye* and *Hammer of the Gods: The Led Zeppelin Saga*)

2. About seven crumpled pieces of paper

3. The offending sandwich half

4. Two drumsticks

5. Three guitar picks

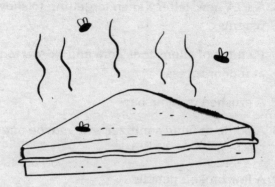

### Two questions that naturally arose when I saw this

1. How could you have forgotten about the sandwich?

2. Are you playing guitar now? (Answer: No. I'm just collecting picks.)

Then I told him that Zora's older brother plays guitar, and he just said, "I know," but he seemed weird about it.

### Eleven things in my backpack right now

1. A binder

2. A spiral notebook

3. One of Kate's hair ties I need to return

4. An eraser shaped like a unicorn, with the top of the horn broken off

5. A PTA newsletter I keep forgetting to show my parents

6. Pictures of aliens that Zora and I drew together at indoor recess

7. A crushed granola bar

8. A bottle of hand sanitizer with *maybe* one squirt left in it

9. A few broken pencils

10. A rock that I found in the driveway and saved because I thought it looked like George Washington

11. A French stamp Mrs. Silva gave me (you know, for my imaginary stamp collection)

### Five things I included in my last letter to Millie

1. A report on the election for fifth-grade class president (which, to the surprise of no one, Zora won by a landslide)

2. A tally of the number of times Amelia has randomly brought up my flying-underwear

kickball incident and started laughing (seven at last count)

3. The news that Mom says I can get my ears pierced if I read fifty books (twenty-five of my choice, twenty-five of hers)

4. A new friendship bracelet in fall colors

5. A hand turkey (you know the kind, where you trace your hand and make it look like a turkey)

**One reason I made my best friend a hand turkey even though we aren't in preschool**

1. It's a tradition. Millie goes to her grandparents' house in California for a week every year at Thanksgiving, and we always trade hand turkeys before she goes. It was Millie's idea; it started the first year we were friends and I was mopey about being away from her for a whole week.

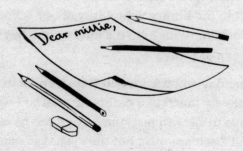

## Four things I did not tell Millie in my letter

1. I overheard my parents talking about bills again
   after I went to bed last night. Mom is emailing
   some of her work friends in the city to try to get
   more assignments, and Dad's going to ask about
   overtime pay at his new job. I don't know why I
   didn't tell Millie, exactly. It's not like she thinks
   we're rich—I mean, she knew we had to move out
   of our first Brooklyn apartment because the rent
   went up. But money is definitely coming up more
   these days, and it just doesn't feel like something I
   want to tell my friends about. (Especially a friend
   like Millie, whose parents have always had the
   same big apartment and take nice vacations every
   year.)

2. I've started going to the school library some
   days at lunchtime to look for the old books Mom
   recommends for the ear-piercing challenge. If
   Kate's there too, I talk to her and help her shelve
   books. (I'm not sure why I didn't tell Millie about
   that. Maybe because we never would have hung
   out in the library voluntarily at our school in
   Brooklyn. With Kate it's kind of fun, but it's hard
   to explain why.)

3. One day when Zora and Kate were both out sick,
   I ate my lunch in a bathroom stall so I wouldn't
   have to sit with just Amelia and the boys. (Charlie
   and Zach are nice, but they just don't make
   enough of a buffer between Amelia and me.)

4. When I heard Amelia on the bus asking Zora if she could be her campaign manager for the class election (and Zora saying, "Sure!"), it made my stomach hurt for the rest of the ride home. (Did *I* want to be the campaign manager? No. But according to my stomach, I guess I didn't want Amelia to do it either.)

### Two things I did not get from Millie before Thanksgiving

1. A letter

2. A hand turkey

She did send a quick email that said, "Sorry I didn't have time to do a turkey this year. Leaving for the airport soon. Happy Thanksgiving!" Hmph. But I was going to try not to let one snoreburger of an email kill my holiday spirit.

### Two reasons I'm excited about Thanksgiving this year

1. We could never host it before because our Brooklyn apartment was too small. But this year we have enough space for the whole family to come, and some will even stay over. (I'm excited about this, but Mom and Dad are kind of freaking out. They're more concerned than usual about how the house looks, and they keep arguing about things like whether they should buy more pillows or ask people to bring their own. They

don't say it, but I know these are just more things they never would have had to worry about if I hadn't made us move.)

2. I get to bunk with my mom's younger sister, Aunt Penelope. (And no matter how crummy I'm feeling about moving, my parents, or Ted, Aunt Penelope is one person who always makes me feel better.)

**Four best feelings**

1. Saturday morning

2. A compliment from someone who's not your parent

3. A compliment on something you don't think you're good at (For example, "Annie, you kicked that ball so far!" I'm still waiting for that one.)

4. Your parents saying, "Let's just order pizza tonight."

### Three worst feelings

---

1. Nausea

2. Getting a splinter (Actually, I don't know if it's getting the splinter that's so bad, or just the idea of a sliver of wood sliding into your skin. Shudder.)

3. Waking up the day after you've gotten bad news (Because at first you've forgotten the bad news and it feels like a regular morning; then your brain slowly reminds you, and it feels like you're hearing it for the first time all over again.)

### Seven things I love about Aunt Penelope (or Aunt Pen, as Ted and I call her)

---

1. She has really long hair—almost to her bottom— although she usually wears it up. When I was little, one of my favorite things to do was watch her twist her hair into a long rope and tie it in a knot. It's so long that it will stay like that with no clip or hair tie or anything.

2. She taught me how to make a quilt for my dolls when I was seven.

3. She's a teacher and she knows everything about books for kids my age. So she always recommends the best ones for me to read.

4. When her house got infested with ladybugs, she

never called an exterminator. She just let them be. So they live on her kitchen ceiling in clusters around the lamp, like sunbathers on a beach.

5. When she visits us, she brings me a container full of ladybugs to live in my old butterfly habitat.

6. She understands what it's like to be a younger sister. Mom tries, but she'll never really know because she never lived it like Aunt Pen and I have.

7. She never says anything about me being quiet or shy.

**Five people who DID say I was shy at Thanksgiving**

1. Grandma Rose

2. Grandma Elaine

3. Grandpa Mac

4. Uncle Dan

5. Aunt Charlene

**Five questions Aunt Pen asked while she was teaching me to knit that night**

1. You know that *I* know that you're not always quiet, right? (Answer: Yes, it's easier to talk with you.)

2. What has been the best part about this new place so far? (Answer: Riding my bike more. And the purple house. Also, Zora and Kate at school are pretty nice. But they aren't as great as Millie. Millie is still my best friend.)

3. What has been the hardest for you? (Answer: Missing Millie. What I didn't say: Feeling like it's my fault that we had to move.)

4. What do you miss about Millie? (Answer: Just hanging out with her. Also writing notes to each other in school.)

5. How do you think Ted likes it here? (Answer: He hates it.)

**Five things Aunt Pen told me about herself then that I never knew before**

---------------------------------------------------------------

1. She was about my age when she and my mom moved to a new town.

2. She decided it was her chance to act like a new person, and she asked everyone to call her Nell. (She thought that was a better nickname than Penny.)

3. One day on the bus someone heard my mom call her Penelope, and all the kids started asking her why she'd lied about her name.

4. For a while there were crazy rumors about her, like the ones that started about me in my old

school (but for Aunt Pen, it was in her *new* school, and the main rumor was that she'd had to lie about her name because Grandpa robbed a bank in their old town and they were on the run).

5. Finally she started playing tennis and made friends that way. And people stopped believing the crazy rumors.

I told her she should tell Ted her story. She said she would do that.

I thought about telling Aunt Pen the crazy rumors that had started about me in Brooklyn, and the reasons people thought I got myself kicked out. But I decided that would only bring back all the icky feelings. Maybe if I didn't talk about the things I messed up in Brooklyn, it would be easier to have a new start in Clover Gap. Besides, there was something bigger on my mind right then.

**One question I asked Aunt Pen while we were knitting**

1. What's a severance agreement? (Her answer, after a long pause: I think you should ask your parents.)

Then she changed the subject and told me that if I missed writing notes to Millie, maybe I should try writing a note to one of my new friends here.

**Five things I told Zora in the note I wrote her Thanksgiving night**

---

1. I got ten new ladybugs from Aunt Penelope.

2. I peeled twenty potatoes.

3. I got the bigger side of the wishbone that Ted and I broke. So I was supposed to get my wish, but of course I couldn't tell her what it was or it wouldn't come true. (Truth: I wished that Millie wouldn't make a new best friend.)

4. Ted broke a glass while he was drumming.

5. I was glad we didn't have school, but I knew I'd be bored starting tomorrow because Aunt Pen was going home in the morning.


I folded the paper and wrote "From A to Z" on the outside.


**Five unexpected things that happened the next day**

---

1. Two of my ladybugs escaped from the habitat and "set up housekeeping," as Grandma Rose called it, on my bedroom ceiling.

2. Grandma Elaine went shopping and bought an area rug to cover the bare plywood spot in our living room. "It's your housewarming gift," she said when Mom told her she shouldn't have.

3. The weather got much warmer than usual for November and I could go outside without a jacket.

4. Zora called and asked if I could ride my bike over to her house. (This is one of my parents' favorite things about Clover Gap too, that we can ride our bikes everywhere.)

5. When I got to Zora's, Amelia was there.

## Five things I have noticed about Amelia

1. Her handwriting is amazing. It should be its own font. And after she writes a word, she'll look back at it and touch it up.

2. She has ten different perfect outfits, and she wears each of them on the same school day on alternating weeks. For example, Monday: kitten sweater and red skirt. Tuesday: black dress, black leggings, silver boots. Wednesday: pink button-down shirt, sparkly leggings. Thursday: ROCK STAR! T-shirt, jean jacket, and tan skirt. Friday: heart sweatshirt and jeans.

3. Her books are always stacked in perfect size order inside her desk.

4. Her pencils are all round (no hexagonal yellow ones) with soft pink erasers.

5. She always carries cherry cough drops with her and pops them like candy. (When I have a cough, Mom makes me take the ones that taste like medicine, and she only lets me have two a day. Not that I argue. Because, like I said, they taste like medicine.)

**Three ways I could tell Amelia was unhappy to see me at Zora's house**

1. When I arrived, Amelia immediately spotted the note for Zora in my bike basket. Without even saying hello, she said, " 'From A to Z'—what's that?"

2. I told her it was a note I wrote for Zora on Thanksgiving, and she rolled her eyes and said, "Is it about Pilgrims or something?"

3. She spent the rest of the afternoon talking to Zora about people I didn't know, and things that happened before I moved to Clover Gap.

I was happy to go home and flop down on my bed with *Finding Someplace* (Aunt Pen's latest book recommendation) and my stuffed animals.

## Top six names for my stuffed animals

1. Dolly Llama

2. Kermit the Dog

3. Joy Kangaroo

4. Disco Pig

5. Menacing Venison

6. Natasha

Ted says these all sound like band names. Mom says that's a compliment coming from him and that I should take it. I think he's just trying to annoy me.

## Weird habits I've broken

1. Biting my fingernails

2. Arranging my stuffed animals in a perfect line across the foot of my bed before going to sleep

3. Wiping my mouth on my shirtsleeve

4. Wearing gloves when I caught fireflies (I was afraid they would shock me.)

5. Running out of the bathroom every time I flushed the toilet (I had a secret fear that a ghost was going to come out of the toilet to replace the water. Crazy, I know.)

## Weird habits I still need to kick

1. When I'm bored, wrapping a hair tightly around my finger until it turns bluish

2. Cracking my knuckles

3. Making all my movements symmetrical (like if I scratch my left ear, I also have to scratch my right one, even if it doesn't itch)

4. Getting a new glass every time I have a drink of water (I actually don't think this is a weird habit, but it drives Mom bananas, so I've told her I'll work on it.)

# DECEMBER

**Four reasons I left lunch early today**

1. The cafeteria reeked of fish sticks and it was starting to make me feel sick.

2. Amelia was droning on about whether she should get candy canes or snowmen painted on her fingernails at her next manicure appointment, and that was starting to make me feel sick too.

3. Zora was preoccupied with writing a birthday wish list to send to her grandparents. (Her winter trip to visit them in Jamaica is coming up, and her grandmother wants gift ideas since she'll be there on her birthday.)

4. I had to go to the library to look for Mom's latest book recommendation, *Dicey's Song*.

### Five people I saw when I got to the library

1. Mrs. Otis (the librarian) quietly typing at her computer

2–4. Three sixth-grade boys whispering in the back corner (I knew two of them were named Lionel and James because they ride my bus and other kids are always saying their names. I didn't know the third kid. I'm quite sure none of them knew me.)

5. Kate shelving books in the biography section

### Three things Kate loud-whispered to me after she saw me

1. Psst! Hey, Annie!

2. Are you here to hang out or to get a book? (Answer: Both, really.)

3. What book?

At this point Mrs. Otis looked up from her computer. So I shuffled over to Kate and told her I was looking for *Dicey's Song.*

"That's by Cynthia Voigt," she said. "Go look in the Vs."

**Two things I saw when I looked in the direction Kate was pointing**

---

1. A tall shelf labeled FICTION S–V

2. The three sixth-grade boys standing directly in front of it

**Eight thoughts I had next**

---

1. Lionel, James, and Boy Whose Name I Don't Know are standing directly in front of the shelf I need to get to.

2. They don't look like they're moving anytime soon.

3. In fact, Boy Whose Name I Don't Know just slid down, leaned against the bottom shelf, and started thumbing through a *World Almanac*.

4. Why is the *World Almanac* in the fiction section?

5. I wonder if Kate mis-shelved it.

6. Never mind about that.

7. I do not want to go over and ask those boys to move so I can look for my book.

8. I will just find another book.

"Actually," I said to Kate, "I just remembered I want to get this one instead." I bent down and grabbed the first book I saw: *The Biography of Dorothy Hamill*.

### Three questions Kate asked next

1. Dorothy Hamill? Who is that? (Answer: She was a famous ice skater in the 1970s. With a famous haircut.)

2. That's really the book you want? (Answer, as I glanced over and saw that the sixth graders were still there: Yes, this is it.)

3. Can you wait here a second? (Answer: Sure, I'll just be reading my book.)

Kate walked over to the fiction shelves, said, "Excuse me, Frank" (to Boy Whose Name I Now Know Is Frank), leaned over, and grabbed a book.

### Four things I appreciated about Kate in that moment

1. She figured out why I didn't want to go over to the fiction shelves.

2. She didn't laugh at me for it.

3. Unlike me, she didn't care about asking sixth-grade boys to move so she could get a book.

4. She actually got me the book I wanted, and I could stop reading about 1970s figure skating.

"Here you go," Kate said as she handed me *Dicey's Song*. "Merry Christmas."

**Three things that would be on my Christmas list if I thought my family could afford them**

1. A cell phone

2. A puppy

3. A canopy bed

**Three more realistic things I am putting on my Christmas list**

1. A landline phone for my room

2. A goldfish

3. My own jar of peanut butter to eat by myself, scoop by scoop (a dream of mine for a long time, though Mom says it's gross)

**Five things I figure I'll really get for Christmas**

1. A sweater

2. Socks

3. Art supplies

4. Maybe the jar of peanut butter

5. Maybe the old-school phone

## Four things I actually got for Christmas

1. A sweater

2. Socks

3. Art supplies

4. Walkie-talkies (from Grandma Elaine)

Hmm. Grandma suggested that Ted and I could use the walkie-talkies to communicate with each other while we were in different parts of the house. I knew that would be tricky, seeing as how Ted was barely talking to me at all. I could tell he almost rolled his eyes when she said that.

## My three biggest Christmas disappointments

1. No phone of any kind

2. No fish

3. Not even any peanut butter (seriously?!)

### Ted's biggest Christmas disappointment

1. No concert tickets

### Mom's biggest Christmas disappointment

1. Aunt Pen couldn't come because she was in London with her friends. (That was one of my disappointments too.)

### Dad's biggest Christmas disappointments

1. He couldn't get the fire in the fireplace just right. He said it was because the wood was damp, but Mom was able to get it going pretty well once she gave it a try.

2. Grandma Elaine gave him a book called *Gardening for Dummies,* and he didn't seem amused by it. It's gotten to be kind of a joke between Mom and Grandma, how Dad is a city kid who doesn't know how to do stuff like build fires and grow plants. Dad laughed along with them at first, but I think he's getting tired of it.

### Dad's pet peeves

1. Empty milk cartons returned to the fridge (usually by Ted)

2. Piles of unopened mail

3. Globs of toothpaste in the bathroom sink

4. Wasting napkins, tissues, printer paper—pretty much waste of any kind of paper product

**Four things I heard that night after I went to my room to draw with my new art supplies**

1. Mom in the kitchen, singing along to "Mele Kalikimaka" with Bing Crosby

2. Dad crumpling up newspapers to put under the logs in the fireplace

3. Ted playing drums upstairs

4. A break in the drumming, then a staticky sound on my walkie-talkie, followed by "Annie, can you hear me?" It was Ted.

### Three things I learned after I told Ted I could hear him

1. Ted is more interested in the walkie-talkies than he first let on (or he's just bored enough to give them a try).

2. Ted is more willing to talk to me over a walkie-talkie than in person (although we were mostly just saying things like "Can you hear me? I'm in the basement" and "Yes, I hear you—I'm upstairs").

3. The walkie-talkies work pretty well.

### Four places we tried the walkie-talkies

1. Ted in his room, me in mine

2. Ted in Mom and Dad's room, me in the bathroom

3. Ted in the living room, me in Mom's office

4. Ted in the basement laundry room, me in the attic

That's when I saw my chance. I climbed into the attic crawl space off Ted's bedroom (with his permission this time), sat down with my legs crossed, and pressed the talk button on the walkie-talkie. "Ted, if you can hear me, can you come here so I can show you something?" He heard me.

**Three things Ted said when I showed him the severance letter**

----------------------------------------------------------------

1. This means that Dad got fired.

2. We moved here because Dad lost his job in Brooklyn. Not because of you.

3. Why didn't they tell us?


"So it wasn't because of me blabbing to Mr. Lawrence?" I asked him.

Ted looked down at the letter again. "No," he said. "Actually, this letter was sent in February, and you didn't talk to Mr. Lawrence until May. Dad wasn't working at all for six months. No wonder they've been even weirder than usual about money."


**Five things Ted and I said in our Christmas email to Aunt Pen**

----------------------------------------------------------------

1. Merry Christmas!

2. We miss you.

3. Did you know Dad lost his job in Brooklyn?

4. Why didn't they tell us?

5. What do we do now?

I asked Ted if he thought we should tell Mom and Dad what we had found. He said he wasn't sure, and that if they didn't tell us, there must be a reason they didn't want us to know. So we waited to hear back from Aunt Pen.

### Five things Aunt Pen said in her December 26 email back to us
---

1. Merry belated Christmas to you, too!

2. I tried to call you yesterday, but I have spotty service here.

3. Did you know today is called Boxing Day in England?

4. I miss you guys too.

5. About the job, like I said . . . I think you should talk to your parents.


I said that meant we were back to square one. Ted said not really, and that if Dad hadn't lost his job, Aunt Pen would have told us we were being ridiculous. Her saying "You should talk to your parents" pretty much meant we were right.

So are we going to talk to them? We still aren't sure.

**Three reasons Ted says he's not sure we should ask Mom and Dad about the letter**

1. They might just be mad that we looked through their papers.

2. What difference does it make? It's not like this will make them move back to Brooklyn.

3. If they'd hide something this big from us, I don't know if I feel like talking to them anyway.

**Two reasons I'm not so sure about asking them either**

1. Same as Ted's first reason. What if we get in trouble for snooping?

2. I'm afraid that we're wrong. I'm afraid they'll say our move had nothing to do with Dad's job, and that I really was the only reason we left Brooklyn.

I'm starting to feel more and more on edge every time I'm around my parents. Maybe because I'm irritated at them for keeping something from us, or maybe because I'm afraid they're trying to protect me from truth I don't want to hear (and maybe a little of both). Either way, winter break is the worst time to feel like you want to get away from your parents, because you're pretty much trapped with them for days on end.

**Five things I've done during the rest of winter break while trying to avoid Mom and Dad**

1. Holed up in my room and knit more of the scarf Aunt Pen helped me start at Thanksgiving.

2. Played video games with Ted in the basement.

3. Watched too much TV for my mother's comfort.

4. Knocked icicles off the gutters with a broomstick (a surprisingly satisfying activity).

5. Written letters to Millie.


**Six things I've told Millie in my letters**

1. Mr. Allbright doesn't give too much homework, and on Fridays he gives assignments like "bake cookies" or "hug a tree."

2. I haven't seen any new movies because the movie theater here doesn't get anything until it's been out forever. Snoreburger.

3. Our house is on a hill, and when it snows, we can sled in the front yard as long as someone stands in the street to make sure no cars are coming.

4. I miss our favorite pizza place in Brooklyn. The pizza here isn't nearly as good—too much tomato sauce, and the crust isn't thin enough.

5. I miss the drugstore on her corner, where the owner always gave us free lollipops.

6. I miss her.

I don't know why I haven't told her anything about the severance letter, or Ted's and my new theories about the move. If we still lived in Brooklyn, I would have told her right away. Something about not being around someone every day makes it harder to explain the things that worry you.

### Four things Millie has written in her letters to me

1. She got a hamster for Hanukkah.

2. She went shopping in Manhattan with her mom and they walked back across the Brooklyn Bridge because the subways were all messed up, and it was FREEZING.

3. All the fifth graders are going camping at Bear Mountain at the end of the school year.

4. There is a new kid in school from France. Her name is Juliette. She is cool.

I want to know more about this cool French Juliette. Was she one of the fork-knife-spoon trio on Halloween? Is she going to be Millie's best friend now? If Millie is going to have a different best friend, who will be mine?

## Four thoughts on best friends

1. They can make you feel safe, like you always have someone to hang out with no matter what.

2. They can make you feel lonely if you suddenly find yourself without them.

3. Maybe it's okay not to have a best friend. Or to have more than one best friend.

4. Maybe you can't get everything you need from one person.

# JANUARY

**Nine reasons I was late to school on the first day back from winter break**

------------------------------------------------------------------------

1. We got a phone call in the morning that the school buses were running late because of icy conditions on the roads.

2. I thought that meant I could take my time getting ready and maybe even go back to bed for a while, but Dad said no, he would drop me off on his way to work. (This was annoying because I was actually *really* looking forward to riding the bus. Have I mentioned that I was ready for some space from my parents?)

3. I couldn't find my water bottle.

4. Mom, who usually helps me find stuff, was on an early conference call with a client and said we could only interrupt her if there was an emergency.

5. Dad said a missing water bottle didn't count as an emergency, so he filled an old water bottle and put it in my lunch box.

6. The cap on the old water bottle was loose, and it leaked all over my backpack.

7. Dad spent about three hours looking for his ID badge for work. (Okay, it was more like ten minutes, but it felt like three hours.)

8. When we got outside, it was so cold that the car wouldn't start.

9. When Dad finally got the car started after five tries, he realized he'd forgotten his coffee thermos and he had to run back inside for it. He came back out just as the bus was passing our driveway. We wound up behind it for most of the drive. I stared out my window as the kids on the bus made stupid faces at us and wrote with their fingers on the steamed-up windows.

By the time we got to school, I wasn't speaking to Dad. (Not that he cared. He was grouchy too, grumbling about how he'd never had to worry about starting the car on cold days in the city.) And I was feeling very ready to be around people outside my family again.

**Five things that actually made me feel worse once I was at school**

---------------------------------------------------------------------

1. Zora told me Mrs. Martin, the bus driver, had given all the kids Hershey's Kisses she had left over from Christmas.

2. Amelia said, "Zora, let's show Annie our watches!" and she took Zora's left wrist and thrust both of their arms toward me so I could see that they had matching watches with lines of little pink elephants marching across the green wristbands.

3. Amelia added, "This was my Christmas present to Zora. My parents got me one too. Elephants have been our favorite animal forever, right, Z?" Zora gave a quiet nod, but she looked a little embarrassed at the way Amelia was making a big deal about the watches.

4. Without thinking, I said, "Really, elephants? I thought cats were Zora's favorite." Zora said, "They are. But I liked elephants when I was little." Amelia looked me straight in the eye and said, "We have both *always* loved elephants."

5. At lunch, while Zora was still waiting in line for her food, Amelia pulled a postcard out of her backpack and said, "You guys have to hear this note Zora sent me from Jamaica. She's so funny." She started to read: " 'Dear Amelia, Thank you

so much for the elephant watch you gave me before I left. I love it! I packed it in my trunk so I could bring it to Jamaica with me. Love, your best friend, Zora.'"

"What's so funny about that?" Kate asked.

"Don't you get it?" Amelia said, like Kate was an idiot. "It's an *elephant* watch, and she said she packed it in her *trunk*?"

"Oh, okay," Kate said, throwing me a sidelong glance. But all I was paying attention to was the postcard. Because as Amelia was sliding it back into her backpack, I caught a glimpse of Zora's sign-off. It just said, "See ya soon, Z." It did *not* say, "Love, your best friend, Zora." Amelia had made that up.

I know all this shouldn't have made me feel crummy, but it did. I had never known kids who gave other kids Christmas presents unless they were in the same family and their parents made them do it. It was like Amelia and Zora had this serious grown-up friendship. And why did Amelia lie about the way Zora signed the postcard? We already knew they had been friends practically since they were born; she didn't have to make stuff up to prove it.

**And three things at school that eventually made me feel better**

1. Zora brought shell bracelets back from Jamaica for me, Amelia, and Kate. Mine had a little

dolphin charm dangling off it, Kate's had a starfish, and Amelia's had a sea horse. (Maybe it was my imagination, but Amelia looked a little disappointed with hers.)

2. During Mr. Allbright's lesson on reflexive pronouns, he asked us which word was grammatically correct, "hisself" or "himself." A few minutes later, Kate passed me a piece of paper. On it she had drawn a coiled-up snake with sunglasses and arched eyebrows, and under it was written "Hisssself." She also wrote, "Hang out after school today?"

3. At lunch I called Mom and asked if I could go home with Kate, and she said it was okay as long as we did homework.

**Weird things I've always wondered**

------------------------------------------------------------------

1. What it would be like to spin with the clothes inside a dryer

2. Who I would be if my parents had married other people

3. Whether people actually see things the same way. Like, do things that look blue to me look red to other people? And if so, how would we ever know?

4. If I had done one thing differently today—like tie

my left shoe before my right one—would it have somehow made my whole life different? Or even changed the world?

## Five things Millie and I used to do on cold days in Brooklyn

----------------------------------------------------------------

1. Go ice skating at the outdoor rink in Prospect Park

2. Find snow in the park that no one had walked in yet, and write our names in it with a stick

3. Sit by my living room window and count how many people slipped on the icy sidewalk

4. Put broken crayons on wax paper on top of the radiator cover in Millie's bedroom and see how long it took for them to melt (We learned the hard way that we had to use wax paper. The rainbow blob stain on the radiator cover was proof of that. Oops.)

5. Read my mom's high school yearbook. I know this sounds boring, but Mom's yearbook is hilarious. Everyone had gigantic hair. Millie liked to quiz me by covering up the names and seeing how many people I could identify. (It was a lot, partly because of my crazy memory, and partly because I had spent many cold and rainy days with that yearbook.)

### Twenty-four things to do after school on a frigid day in Clover Gap

-----------------------------------------------------------------

1. Try not to fall off the bus seat, which is too crowded because everyone is carrying backpacks and wearing parkas.

2. Walk from the bus stop using little chicken steps so you don't slip on the ice.

3. Write your name in the snow—or make a snow angel—just about anywhere you want. (There's a lot more undisturbed snow in Clover Gap than there was in Prospect Park.)

4. If you are lucky, you will be with a friend like Kate, and she will help you make snowballs to use against the older neighbor kids who got home before you did.

5. Yell, "RUN!" to Kate when she reaches the steps in front of her house, because the older kids are hiding behind a bush and throwing snowballs.

6. Throw snowballs back at the offending kids and run inside, slamming the door behind you.

7. Watch through the window as offending kids restock their snowballs for later.

8. Poke around in Kate's pantry until you find satisfactory snacks.

9. Go outside and collect a bowl full of clean snow.

10. Make snow cream. (Mix the snow with cream, sugar, and vanilla. I had never tried this, probably because clean snow was harder to come by in Brooklyn.)

11. Eat snow cream.

12. Discuss different businesses you could start.

13. Decide that best options for new businesses are used-book store and private-investigator service.

14. Have a third snack.

15. Hear Kate's babysitter's fifth reminder about homework.

16. Start homework.

17. Talk about who in our class has crushes on whom. (If Mr. Allbright were reading this, he would be happy that I remembered to use "whom" there.)

18. Do a little more homework.

19. Ask Kate questions about people in school (more on that later).

20. Practice writing our names in bubble letters.

21. Say goodbye to Kate because her babysitter says we aren't getting enough homework done and it's time to leave.

22. Call Mom and ask her to pick me up.

23. Go home and finish homework.

24. Bug older brother.

One good thing about that severance letter: after I showed it to Ted, he blamed me a lot less for our move to Clover Gap. I was definitely feeling more and more awkward around my parents as I wondered what they weren't telling us (like how serious were our money problems, really, and were things okay with their jobs now?). But at least things between Ted and me were almost back to normal. Which meant we talked more, and I also wasn't afraid to bug him like I used to.

**Ten great ways to annoy an older brother**

1. If his bedroom door is closed, stand in the doorway with your arms and legs braced against the sides of the door frame. When he opens the door, you will give him a heart attack. It's worth the wait.

2. Sing. Sing whatever you want. Anything will annoy him as long as it's coming from you.

3. If possible, change the song lyrics so they involve a girl you suspect he likes.

4. Sit directly beside him when he's watching TV.

5. Stand in front of the screen while he's playing a video game.

6. Look at him during meals.

7. Call him a cute nickname. (In this case it works particularly well, since Ted hates his cute nickname, which, of course, is "Teddy.")

8. Lean ever so slightly toward his side of the backseat when you're in the car.

9. Put heart stickers on his notebooks.

10. Mimic everything he says. (Sure, it's immature, but so are brothers.)

### Five things I like about Kate

1. She kept humming even after the flying-underwear incident.

2. She taught me the sign-language alphabet she learned when she was in the play *The Miracle Worker,* and she uses it to send me secret messages across the classroom (like "B-O-R-I-

N-G," so I taught her "S-N-O-R-E-B-U-R-G-E-R").

3. Like me, she isn't great at kickball, but she doesn't seem to care.

4. Also like me, she notices a lot about other people (which comes in handy when I have questions about kids at school).

5. She asks me a lot of questions about Brooklyn—what was my school like, did I ride the subway, who were my friends there. It's easy to talk to her.

## Three questions I asked Kate after school

1. Why is Zach always jumping up and trying to touch the tops of door frames? (Answer: He has a younger brother who's grown an inch taller than him in the past year. I think Zach hopes all the jumping will help him grow.)

2. Why does Charlie wear hats all the time? (Answer: Not sure. He might be insecure about his ears.)

3. Does Amelia not like me? (Answer: She doesn't *not* like you. But she and Zora have been friends for a long time. Amelia can be possessive of her.) That one I was starting to figure out for myself, but it was good to hear it from someone else.

**Four things I imagine would count as big problems for Amelia**

-----------------------------------------

1. Round-pencil shortage

2. Late Monday night, discovering her Tuesday outfit is in the dirty laundry

3. Stubbed toe

4. Chipped nail polish

**Four things that are currently big problems for me**

-----------------------------------------

1. Worrying that Amelia hates me

2. Worrying that my parents will always be stressed about money

3. Wondering why my parents lied about the reason we moved here, and feeling like I can't trust them

4. Making sure I have enough friends

**Three dreams I have about Brooklyn**

-----------------------------------------

1. I discover a secret panel in my old bedroom closet that opens into a big house with a backyard.

2. I am playing wall ball in my old school playground when the wall disappears, and standing behind it are all the kids in my new class. Also, the ball turns into a gigantic pair of underwear.

3. I am having a fight with Millie. The fight is about something stupid, like who has more freckles, and it makes me feel so frustrated that I want to scream. When I wake up, the feeling lasts even though the dream is over, and I still feel mad at Millie for about half an hour.

**Five things I miss about Millie**

----------------------------------------------------------

1. The way she usually knew what I was thinking without me having to say it

2. The way we passed notes to each other, on pages of a marble notebook. When one notebook was full, we would start a new one. We took turns keeping them when they were finished.

3. Her funny made-up words, like "nao!" (instead of "no!") or "VV?!" which meant she was surprised.

4. She never minded that I was quiet. She said, "Quiet people are interesting."

5. She didn't think it was weird that I remembered everything about everyone.

I have done pretty well with my vow to keep my observation and memory powers to myself here. But sometimes I forget. Like one day Amelia asked me if she could borrow a pencil, and I said, "Sure, but I only have regular yellow ones." She asked me why that would matter, and without thinking I said, "Well, I know you only use round ones."

"No I don't," she said, her eyes getting narrow. Then she turned away and borrowed a pencil from Kate instead. A round one.

# FEBRUARY

**Three things a person wonders before her first
Valentine's Day in a new school**

-------------------------------------------------------------

1. Do fifth graders even do anything for Valentine's
   Day here?

2. If they do, what do they give each other? Cards?
   Candy? Pencils?

3. And if my class does celebrate it, should I give
   something to everyone? Or just the girls?

**Three people who answered my questions**

-------------------------------------------------------------

1. Mr. Allbright, who sent home a letter that said, "If
   you are going to bring in valentines, make sure
   you have one for every student in the class."

2. Zora, who said, "Yes, bring them! And don't forget
   candy. Mr. A will probably give us pencils, but
   kids give each other candy."

3. Kate, who chimed in on Zora's advice: "Most kids just bring in a little candy bar for each person in the class. You can write the names on the wrappers and then you don't have to do cheesy cards."

**Four things I got for Valentine's Day at school**

---

1. Eight mini packs of Skittles

2. Seven packets of Fun Dip

3. Ten miniature chocolate bars

4. Two pencils

The pencils were from Mr. Allbright. They were round, which I think I saw Amelia noting with satisfaction.

**Four surprising things about Valentine's Day at school**

---

1. Everyone actually brought something. Even the boys. (By fourth grade at my old school, half the boys weren't doing the valentine thing anymore.)

2. Charlie just gave Zora a small bag of Skittles, like he gave everyone else. Guess he didn't want to be *too* obvious about his crush. Or maybe the crush is over?

3. Mr. A let us eat candy.

4. It was kind of fun. (No one said a word about pronouns, state capitals, or word problems all afternoon. We doodled on paper hearts and talked to our friends while we munched on chocolate. All in all, not a bad school day.)

**One thing about Valentine's Day that was not particularly surprising. Or fun.**

----------------------------------------------------------------

1. When Amelia saw the little packets of Red Hots I was giving everyone, she said, "Oh, you like those? I think they're way too spicy. I'm surprised you didn't give Zora a personalized present. Seems like you always remember everything she likes."

"I'll take them," Zora said. "I actually love Red Hots. That's something else you can remember."

**Three things I felt like doing in that moment**

----------------------------------------------------------------

1. Hugging Zora

2. Breaking all of Amelia's perfect pencils in half

3. Fleeing the classroom. How did Amelia know I remembered stuff about Zora? I was being so careful about not showing my memory. Did Amelia know I actually remembered stuff about *everyone*?

### One thing I did instead
----------------------------------------------------------------

1. Turned to Zora and said, "My dad melts these and makes red-hot candy apples. You should come over and do it with us sometime."

Zora's eyes got wide and she said she definitely wanted to try that. Amelia was behind me, so I couldn't see her eyes, but I could feel the lasers they were shooting through the back of my head.

What I didn't mention was that Dad had barely cooked at all since we'd moved here, so I wasn't sure if I'd be able to make good on that offer anytime soon. Even though he'd been so excited for our big kitchen, he'd been working too much to use it. When the weather was warmer, he was always out at the job site. Now that it was winter, the construction had slowed down, but his office hours were longer because he and the other engineers had to plan for spring. I knew the red-hot apples might have to wait.

### Two valentines waiting for me at home
----------------------------------------------------------------

1. A box of chocolates from Grandma Elaine

2. Heart-shaped earrings from Aunt Pen, with a note that said, "Your mom told me about your book challenge. Here's some extra motivation!"

**Two things I should have said after Mom handed me those presents**

1. Wasn't that nice of them?

2. Happy Valentine's Day, Mom!

**One thing I should not have said**

1. Well, isn't it nice that *someone* in this family gave me something for Valentine's Day?!

I *should not* have said that. But I did.

**Two things Mom did next**

1. Jerked her thumb in the direction of the dining room

2. Stomped into her office and slammed the door

**Two things I found in the dining room**

1. Flowers from Dad

2. A book of poems from Mom

**Two things I said after I knocked on the office door**

1. Sorry about that.

2. Thanks for the book.

Mom just mumbled "You're welcome" and said she had to call a client. I stood by the door for a while, but I never heard her on the phone. I couldn't remember the last time I'd hung out with her in her office and watched her work.

### Two reasons I think Mom likes to hole up in her office

1. She can get away from Ted and me when we're snippy the way I just was.

2. It's easier to keep secrets from your kids when you aren't around them.

Either way, I guess I'm not the only one who needs space these days. Finally I turned and went up to my room. I took Aunt Pen's earrings with me so I could hold them up and imagine how they'd look once my ears were pierced.

### Four thoughts about getting my ears pierced

1. It's time already! (I haven't done a scientific survey, but I'm pretty sure about 90 percent of girls my age have pierced ears. At least, that's the statistic I keep giving Mom, and I'm sticking to it.)

2. Once I'm allowed to take out my first little piercing studs, I want to get peace signs. Or pandas. Or both.

3. I wonder how much it will hurt.

4. But I don't really care. Mom says I've always had a high pain threshold, which is good for someone who has as many mishaps as I do.

**Four unexpected mishap-related injuries (yes, these have all happened to me)**

1. Jam your finger on a basketball

2. Staple your thumb

3. Chip a tooth while opening a plastic container with your mouth

4. And, most recently . . . trip while holding a pencil with the tip pointing up, causing you to jam the pencil into your arm

**Twelve things that happened after I jammed the pencil into my arm**

1. My arm started bleeding.

2. Mr. Allbright told me to go to the nurse.

3. He told Amelia to go with me.

4. Amelia stood up to come with me, but she looked a little unsteady.

5. "I just don't do so well with blood," she told me as we stepped into the hallway.

6. I told her she could go back if she wanted and I could go to the nurse's office by myself.

7. She said, "No, I'll be okay."

8. By the time we got to the nurse's office, Amelia looked pretty green.

9. Nurse Taylor cleaned off "the puncture site," as she called it, and gave me a Band-Aid while Amelia watched from the doorway.

10. Nurse Taylor told me that I would have a tiny gray mark on my arm . . . for the rest of my life. "It's like a little tattoo," she said. "See, I have one on my hand from when I was in third grade."

11. And with that, Amelia leaned over Nurse Taylor's sink and threw up.

12. Nurse Taylor sent me back to the classroom with a note for Mr. Allbright explaining why I was returning and Amelia wasn't. I gave him the note because I had to, but I promised myself that I wouldn't share this story with anyone else. I already knew Amelia wasn't crazy about me, and it wouldn't help matters much if I blabbed about her getting sick (even if it would have been fun to share an Amelia upchuck story).

**Four questions Kate asked me when she came over after school that day**

1. Why didn't Amelia come back to class after she went to the nurse with you? (Answer: Um, I think she went home.)

2. Why? (Answer: Well . . . I think she spilled something on her Thursday skirt.)

3. What's a Thursday skirt? (Answer: You know . . . the skirt she wears on Thursdays.)

4. What are you talking about? (Answer: Never mind. Do you want a snack?)

Kate gave me a weird look for a second, but luckily the food seemed to distract her. I'd been so focused on keeping Amelia's vomit secret that I'd almost let it slip that I'd memorized her outfit rotation (and that I privately thought of her tan skirt as the "Thursday skirt"—well, every other Thursday, but you know what I mean).

**Nine things I have observed since moving here that I am pretending not to remember**

1. Zora's brother Marcus (age thirteen) watching *The Fresh Beat Band* by himself one day when I was at their house

2. Kate's collection of My Little Pony board books

3. Zach taking one of Charlie's cookies at lunch one day and slipping it into his coat pocket while Charlie was looking the other way

4. Amelia's outfit rotation

5. Zora's habit of sticking her tongue out while she writes

6. Zora's initials inside a heart on the bottom of Charlie's sneaker (either the heart is old, or the crush is still going)

7. Mr. Allbright checking his hair in the mirror every Friday after the last bell rings

8. Mr. Allbright laughing and chatting with Nurse Taylor by her car last Friday afternoon

9. Amelia losing her lunch in the nurse's office

I know it might just seem like good manners that I don't repeat these things, but come on—how tempting is it to tell *someone* about my Allbright-Taylor theory? But I learned my lesson, and I'm keeping my mouth shut.

### Five things I worry would happen if I told anyone about any of the above

1. Whoever I told (probably Kate or Zora) wouldn't be able to keep the secret.

2. I might get someone in trouble without meaning to.

3. I might get myself in trouble without meaning to.

4. People would think I was a weirdo for noticing and remembering so much.

5. I'm already "the new kid"; I don't want to be "the freaky spy kid," too. I'm really ready to just be "a kid."

**But there is one thing I'm REALLY tired of keeping my mouth shut about**

-----------------------------------------------------------------

1. The severance letter

It's getting to be too much. The more Ted and I watch Dad try to figure things out in Clover Gap, the clearer it is that even though he tried to psych us up about living here, he actually never wanted to leave the city. We must have left only because he couldn't find another job in New York.

**Four things Dad seems clueless about in Clover Gap**

-----------------------------------------------------------------

1. Building fires in the fireplace

2. Taking care of house stuff like kitchen drains, clogged gutters, and leaky ceilings (basically anything the building super did for us in Brooklyn)

3. Driving (Because Dad grew up in the city, he

walked or took subways everywhere and almost never had to drive. Since we've lived here, he's had a couple of near misses with parked cars and telephone poles. Mom usually drives if we have to go anywhere far.)

4. Waving (I know this sounds like a dumb one, but everyone waves at people they pass on the street here, whether they know them or not. Mom thinks it's nice. Dad thinks it's weird and he claims he never remembers to do it. Then Mom says he's just being rude.)

So we've been starting to think he never really wanted to move to Clover Gap, and that we came here for some reason they aren't telling us . . . like because Dad lost his job.

I finally went to Ted and told him I thought it was time to confront Mom and Dad about it. Just then, Mom walked into Ted's room.

**Three things Mom asked after she plopped onto Ted's desk chair**

1. Have you guys finished your homework? (Our answer: Yes.)

2. Whose turn is it to set the table tonight? (Ted's answer: Mine.)

3. And then, maybe because we seemed weirdly cooperative: Everything okay with you two?


**Three things Ted said then**

1. Why didn't you tell us Dad lost his old job?

2. Annie thought us moving was all her fault. Because of Mr. Lawrence and the dry cleaner.

3. And if Dad lost his job way back in February, what was he doing all those months when we thought he was going to work?


**Places we all looked next**

1. Ted: at Mom

2. Mom: at me

3. Me: at the floor


Then Mom started crying.

**Four times I have seen my mother cry**

- - - - - - - - - - - - - - - - - - - - - - - - - - - - - - - - - - - - - - - - - - - - - - - - - - - - -

1. When her grandma died

2. My preschool graduation

3. When Ted and I fought for three solid hours one day after we'd all been snowed in for almost a week

4. When she heard that I thought we moved because of me

"Annie, I am so sorry. We really have to talk," she said once she stopped crying. So that night after Dad got home from work, we did.

**Seven things Dad talked about at dinner that night**

- - - - - - - - - - - - - - - - - - - - - - - - - - - - - - - - - - - - - - - - - - - - - - - - - - - - -

1. We did not move because of me.

2. He lost his job in Brooklyn because his engineering firm was having money problems. They hadn't booked enough projects, and they had to let people go.

3. He didn't tell us because he didn't want us to worry.

4. He still spent a lot of time going into Manhattan and looking for a new job, or meeting friends who might know about job leads . . . which is why we didn't clue in to the fact that he was actually

unemployed. (He admitted that he also went for a lot of long walks and saw a couple of movies.)

5. It's true that he and Mom (okay, mostly Mom) had thought of moving out of the city, and luckily he finally found the highway job out here. (But the pay is less, and his bosses aren't sure if they'll keep Dad on once the highway is finished. So we still need to be careful about money.)

6. Small-town life is definitely proving to be an adjustment for him, but he is trying to focus more on the good things about it, like growing flowers in the yard and inviting people over to grill. (This wasn't the most convincing evidence, given that it was February, but I could tell he felt like he needed to give examples, maybe to convince himself as much as anyone else.)

7. Please don't keep your worries from us (like thinking you caused the family to move). We always want you to share what's on your mind.

**One pretty smart point Ted had after that**

--------------------------------------------------------------------

1. But you guys didn't share what was on *your* mind. Why do you expect us to tell you stuff when you didn't tell us about losing your job?

**Two things Dad admitted**

1. I'm sorry.

2. You're right.

**Three things I asked Dad after Mom recruited Ted to help her clean up in the kitchen**

1. Why did you pretend you wanted to move here just for fun? (Answer: Moving out of the city is something your mom has really wanted to try for a while. I thought it was important for her that we all try to like it.)

2. Did you know I thought the whole move was all because of me? (Answer: I honestly had no idea. If I had, I never would have let you go on thinking that.)

3. So, you're trying to be happy in Clover Gap for Mom . . . but you *don't* actually like it? (Answer: Some days yes, some days no. But there were good days and bad days in Brooklyn too. I still *want* to like it here, and that's half the battle.)

"I want to like it here too," I said. "Most days now, I think I do."

"Well," he said, reaching over to tuck my hair behind my ear, "thanks for saying so. Knowing that goes a long way toward helping *me* like it."

**One last question I asked, after Mom and Ted returned (Mom was carrying a plate of cookies, even though it wasn't dessert night)**

---

1. Will we ever move back to Brooklyn?

Up until now, even though he'd been saying some brave stuff, Ted was mostly looking down, like he was talking to his food. But when I asked that last question, Ted's head popped up and he looked right at Mom and Dad. He had obviously been wondering the same thing.

**One answer Mom gave that really didn't satisfy anyone**

---

1. We don't know. But why don't we see how things go here? After a while, Clover Gap might really feel like home to us.

Dad and Ted both seemed really interested in their cookies at that point. I could tell no one could think of a good thing to say next.

**In the spirit of honesty (and lightening the mood), one thing I told them was on my mind right then**

---

1. I stabbed myself with a pencil today, and now I have a tiny tattoo.

**Four things I told Millie in my email to her that night**

---

1. Did you know that if you poke yourself hard enough with a pencil, it leaves a mark that will be there for the rest of your life? Don't try this yourself; I'll show you my mark next time I see you.

2. There's a lot of snow here.

3. Kate is an amazing snowball maker. She helped me retaliate when Ted attacked us.

4. So . . . guess what. We found out that the *real* reason we left Brooklyn was that my dad lost his job there. He didn't tell us because he didn't want us to worry. And Mom was seriously into trying out small-town life, so she wanted to come here. Anyway, point is . . . it really *wasn't* my fault that we moved.


Even though this was big news, I didn't want to call Millie and have anyone overhear our conversation. So I sent the email, and I spent about half an hour after that listening for the ding that meant she had written me back. Finally Mom made me get ready for bed.

**Five things that happened between Amelia and me at school the day after the pencil incident**

---

1. When we were alone in the coatroom, I asked her how she was feeling.

2. She said, "Fine. Why?" in a flat voice.

3. "You know, because you were sick yesterday," I answered.

4. She replied, "I don't know what you're talking about."

5. "Right," I answered. "Never mind."

Like I said, I wasn't going to tell anyone about Amelia throwing up. But I didn't realize I'd have to pretend it didn't happen with Amelia herself. I'm not sure what the big deal is. I mean, throw-up happens.

### Five inconvenient places I have vomited

1. In the car on the way to my dad's cousin's wedding

2. On the "new book" cart at the public library

3. On my babysitter's shoes

4. At my dad's office on Take Your Kids to Work Day

5. In the prize box at the dentist's office

As you can see, this is something I had a bit of experience with when I was younger. Luckily, it doesn't happen much anymore. But I guess my "upchuck years," as Dad calls them, made me get used to the idea of throwing up. I used to worry a lot that it was going to happen again at any minute. But now that my stomach has settled down, there are other worries that keep me awake at night.

# MARCH

**Nine things I worry about when I'm trying to fall asleep**

---------------------------------------------------------------

1. Kickball starting again when the weather gets warm

2. Mysterious noises (There are way more mysterious night noises in Clover Gap than there were in Brooklyn. And of course I secretly suspect bears.)

3. That Millie is mad at me (She still hasn't responded to my email about Dad's job. Did she not get it? Did I annoy her when I said Kate was a great snowball maker? What is going on?)

4. That Amelia will decide to convince Zora that she shouldn't be friends with me

5. That my parents won't be able to afford the things we need, and that they'll argue about it, and that the house will fall apart because everything is too expensive to fix

6. That Dad's highway job will never end, and we'll stay in Clover Gap forever, and Ted will always be miserable, and I'll never have a real best friend again

7. That Dad's highway job *will* end soon, and then we'll *really* have money problems

8. That if we move back to Brooklyn, I won't have a best friend there, either, because Millie seems to be moving on

9. Other big things, like people who are treated unfairly. I don't know if other kids my age worry about stuff like this. No one really talks about it, so it's hard to tell. But stories like the one about Zora's mom and the pool party go through my head over and over again.

When I told Mom about that one, I could tell she wasn't really sure what to say.

**Four things Mom said when I told her Zora's mom's story**

---------------------------------------------------------------

1. You're right. That is awful.

2. Unfortunately, that kind of thing used to be pretty common.

3. Actually, it still happens more than you'd think.

4. What did you say when Zora told you?

I told Mom that I'd said I thought it was awful, and that Zora had agreed but hadn't seemed as shocked as I was. "It's probably a story she's known for a long time," Mom said.

"But I'm guessing it's still hurtful for her family."

### One other worry that keeps me awake at night
------------------------------------------------------------

1. Coming up with escape routes in the event of a fire

### Three things I would save in a fire
------------------------------------------------------------

Today Mr. Allbright asked us to write about what we would save if our house was on fire and we had to get out fast and could only grab one thing. (His answer: a pocketknife his grandfather gave him.) That assignment stressed me out. When I was in third grade, firefighters came to my school in Brooklyn to talk about fire safety, and one thing they kept repeating was "Do not worry about saving any of your stuff! You can get new toys and clothes, but not a new you!" I guess Mr. Allbright never got that talk. And now that he has asked about it, I imagine that I'll be standing in my smoky room, thinking, "What should I save?" and I'll forget to climb out the window.

But since you asked, Mr. Allbright, here's what I would save:

1. My stuffed panda, Natasha (I've had Natasha the longest. I know I'd feel bad about not saving the others, but I'm picturing the smoky room and I know I'd have to make tough choices.)

2. The locket Aunt Pen gave me for my last birthday

3. My book of lists

**Three things Amelia would save in a fire**

1. Her cashmere sweater

2. Her heart-shaped jewelry box

3. Her photo albums

**Two things Kate would save in a fire**

1. The copy of *The Secret Garden* her grandma gave her

2. Her glasses (She is very practical)

**Three things Charlie would save in a fire**

--------------------------------------------------------

1. His fedora

2. His Lego *Millennium Falcon*

3. His Han Solo T-shirt


**Four things Zach would save in a fire**

--------------------------------------------------------

1. His Lego Death Star

2. His Darth Vader shirt (definitely a theme here)

3. His catcher's mitt

4. His grandpa's army medals

**Two things Zora would save in a fire**

--------------------------------------------------------

1. Her fluffy purple pillow (because she can't sleep without it)

2. Her neighborhood map


She has worked on her map for years, adding to it whenever she discovers a cool new or secret place. She says she can't make a copy of it because she doesn't want it to "fall into the wrong hands."

**Five important landmarks on Zora's map of the neighborhood**

1. Skeleton Hill, the best sledding hill in Clover Gap

2. Hollow Oak, the best place to leave secret notes and treasures like arrowhead rocks

3. Pond Fort, a small, grassy place on the banks of the pond. It's hidden from view by the willow trees that bend over it.

4. The Giant Hole, a pit in the middle of Mr. and Mrs. Sutter's Y-shaped driveway. The hole is in the spot where the Y forks, and it has a big utility pole coming out of it. All the neighborhood kids make a game out of seeing if they can ride their bikes past the Giant Hole and reach out and touch the utility pole without falling in.

5. The rock stream in the woods behind her house


**Four cool things about the rock stream in winter**

1. It's shallow enough that it freezes pretty quickly.

2. After a light snowfall, if you look closely, you can see the shapes of the individual snowflakes on the ice.

3. When the ice is thick, the neighborhood kids have sliding races on it.

4. When the ice is thin, you can see little fish swimming just beneath it.

**Three reasons Zora was determined to catch a fish in the rock stream**

1. She had just watched a TV show about ice fishing and wanted to try it out.

2. Marcus told her he didn't think she could do it.

3. She wanted me to have a pet, and she couldn't bring a fish into her house or her cat would eat it right away. (I didn't tell her that I'd asked for a fish for Christmas and hadn't gotten one.)

**How I came to own Rocky, my pet fish**

1. Zora and I used loose rocks from the creek bank to pound a hole in the ice.

2. This scared away all the nearby fish, so we had to sit on a big rock poking out of the stream for a while—and wait.

3. Zora dipped a bent clothes hanger with a piece of crusty bread on the end of it into the water.

4. Then we waited some more.

5. And a little more.

6. Still more waiting.

7. Finally a few fish started to swim our way.

8. Zora handed me the wire and picked up a big red plastic cup.

9. Incredibly, one little fish started nibbling at the bread.

10. Then another one joined him, and another.

11. Zora sneaked up on the fish with the red cup and pounced.

12. She scooped the cup into the water, catching the three fish.

13. At the same time, she lost her balance and crashed through the ice.

14. All the fish in the water darted away.

15. "Grab the cup!" Zora yelled at me.

16. I grabbed the cup with the three little fish still inside and helped Zora out of the water, which, luckily, was only a few inches deep.

17. We headed back to Zora's house, where we got

    a. Dry clothes for Zora

    b. A talking-to from Zora's mom about being very careful on the ice

18. I took the fish home and put them in a big pickle jar.

19. Mom told me we could go to the pet store over the weekend to get a proper fishbowl.

20. Two of the fish died overnight before I could think of names for them.

21. One of the fish stuck around, and I named him Rocky, after the stream where I found him. So I finally got a fish after all. I wasn't going to get too attached to him, though. Two things I'd learned from Millie: fish and friendships are unpredictable.

Not long after that, the ice started to melt, and spring was on its way. The fish were harder to catch in the warm weather, so we stopped trying. Now our favorite thing to do was ride our bikes, especially around the Giant Hole in the Sutters' driveway.

# APRIL

**Three names Aunt Penelope said when I emailed her
and told her to guess who fell into the Giant Hole**

-----------------------------------------------------------------

1. Annie

2. Annie

3. Annie 😊

Yes, it was me. I was still a little annoyed that Aunt
Pen was so sure of herself, though.

**My pet peeves**

-----------------------------------------------------------------

1. Ted's drumming

2. People dotting their *i*'s with circles or hearts

I think that's it. Maybe I'll have more when I'm older.

### Five things I learned about the Giant Hole

---

1. It's been in the fork of the Sutters' Y driveway for years, ever since the town of Clover Gap used it as an access point for some underground water-main repairs.

2. Mr. and Mrs. Sutter wanted to have it filled in a long time ago, but their kids (who are now in college) had already created the ride-past-the-hole-and-see-if-you-can-touch-the-pole-without-falling-in game, so they (the kids) talked them out of it.

3. It actually is pretty giant. I mean, my bike and my whole body both fit into it, and the ground was still about a foot above my head.

4. The walls of the giant hole are concrete, and lots of people have declared their love in graffiti there. Lots of people have drawn some pretty gross pictures there too.

5. Lucky for me, there were metal rungs on one wall so I could climb out.

### Three bad things that came from me falling into the hole

---

1. Split and bloody lip (which luckily did not require stitches)

2. Ripped jeans

3. Zora had to go back to both of our houses and get Ted and Marcus, because we couldn't get my bike out of the hole ourselves. (It was in pretty deep, and I wasn't much help since I was holding a tissue against my lip to get it to stop bleeding.) Zora decided it was a three-person job. But we knew Ted and Marcus would laugh.

**Three unsurprising things that Ted and Marcus did when they got to the hole**

1. Laughed. A lot.

2. Asked us what we would give them if they rescued the bike (Answer: Two items of their choosing out of our secret candy stashes.)

3. Acted really tough and strong when they were able to lift out the bike

**Three surprising things that Ted and Marcus did when they got to the hole**

1. Gave me a tissue to stop my lip from bleeding (Ted)

2. Checked my bike for dings and scratches (Marcus)

3. Started talking to each other about drumming (Ted and Marcus had met before and kind of grunted at each other in that way that boys do.)

But this time Marcus noticed Ted's drumsticks sticking out of his back jeans pocket, and he asked him about his drums. Since Ted could talk forever about his drums, and Marcus is really into music too, they didn't pay any attention to Zora and me after that, which was fine with us.

## Three things that were different at dinner that night

1. Dad seemed happier. He said wildflowers were starting to bloom in the median on one of the new stretches of the highway he was working on. He hummed while he set the table, and he was full of ideas for the yard (bird feeders, hammocks, etc.). He also said Zora's dad was going to lend him his chain saw so he could cut back some dead branches on our maple tree. (Dad was excited about this; Mom looked nervous.)

2. I could only eat mashed potatoes and applesauce because my lip was so banged up.

3. Ted was super chatty.

## Four things Ted told us about Marcus

1. Marcus is a really good guitar player. (Ted heard him play the national anthem in a pep rally at school.)

2. Marcus wants to start a band.

3. They need a drummer.

4. Marcus said Ted can play for them in their garage this weekend to see if they can "jam."

### Two emails in my inbox that night

1. One from Aunt Pen, asking how I was recovering from my bike ride into the hole

2. One from Millie (almost two months after I had last emailed her) saying just the following:

   a. That's a crazy story about your dad's job.

   b. Even crazier about your pencil mark.

   c. Gotta go; I'm going to the movies with Juliette and Charlotte.

Hardly the shocked reaction I was expecting. Instead, it was my turn to be shocked. She took TWO MONTHS to respond to me?! And she was going to the movies with Juliette . . . and Charlotte? Charlotte Devlin, my second-grade peanut-butter-cracker nemesis?!

### Three things I wrote back to Millie right away

1. Wow, I was starting to think you'd forgotten about me!

2. What movie are you seeing?

3. Are you going with Charlotte *Devlin?*

I wasn't going to say more than that. Not yet. Maybe it wasn't Charlotte Devlin. I didn't know any other Charlottes in Brooklyn . . . but it was certainly possible there was a Brooklyn Charlotte I'd never met. It was a pretty popular name, after all. So I would wait for Millie's response. I didn't want to start a fight.

**Two fights I am trying to forget**

1. Zora's fight with Amelia

2. Zach and Charlie's fight immediately following it

**Why Zora fought with Amelia**

1. At lunch the day after the Giant Hole accident, Amelia asked what happened to my lip.

2. I told her about riding my bike into the hole.

3. Amelia laughed and said, "It serves you right. I can't believe you guys still do that anyway."

**Four things that happened next**

1. Zora slammed down her thermos and said, "Amelia, what is your problem?"

2. Amelia said that she didn't have a problem, and

then added, "But obviously you guys do if you still ride your bikes in circles and play that game with the pole like you're second graders."

3. Zora got quiet for a minute. Then she said, "Amelia, I think you're just jealous because you still don't even know how to ride a bike."

4. Amelia's eyes filled with tears as she grabbed her lunch box and ran from the cafeteria.


## Why Zach fought with Charlie

1. After Amelia ran out, Zach said, "What did you have to say that for, Zora? You know she's embarrassed that she can't ride a bike. That's supposed to be secret."

2. Then Charlie jumped in: "Leave her alone, Zach. Amelia started it."

3. Zach said, "Ugh, Charlie, you're just taking Zora's side because you have a crush on her."


## Five things that happened next

1. Charlie slugged Zach in the arm.

2. Zach slugged Charlie back.

3. Charlie tackled Zach to the floor.

4. From that point on, it was hard to tell what

was happening. But there was definitely lots of punching and kicking.

5. Miss T, one of the lunch aides, pulled them apart and sent them to the assistant principal.

**Four things to know about Mr. Hoover, the assistant principal**

---

1. He never talks unless he absolutely has to, and he has a really deep voice.

2. He is big. "Big" meaning tall, but also meaning he has a belly that is so big that the kids joke that his neckties are parallel to the ground.

3. He is in charge of discipline at the school.

4. If you get called to his office, it almost always means you're in trouble.

So imagine everyone's surprise when the school secretary came on over the intercom and asked for me to come to Mr. Hoover's office. (I think the class's exact words were "Ooooooooh, Annie's in TROUBLE!")

### Three things Mr. Hoover asked when I got to his office

1. Are you friends with Zach and Charlie? (Answer: Yes.)

2. Did you see their fight in the cafeteria? (Answer: Yes.)

3. Can you please tell me everything you remember that happened? (Answer: Um, okay.)

### What I actually remember that happened

Everything, of course. In addition to what happened between Zora and Amelia, I also remember that . . .

1. Zach defended Amelia.

2. Charlie defended Zora.

3. Charlie threw the first punch.

4. Zach was kind of asking for it.

5. Charlie actually does have a crush on Zora.

6. Zora kept yelling, "Guys! Guys!" the whole time.

7. Charlie's potato chips fell to the floor.

8. Zach put his elbow in some applesauce.

9. Zach's Darth Vader shirt got ripped.

10. Both boys cursed.


You get the picture. I remembered a lot, as usual.


### What I told Mr. Hoover I remembered

1. Charlie and Zach got into a fight.

2. I don't know who started it.


### Why I am trying to forget these fights

1. Charlie and Zach are my friends.

2. Even if they weren't, I can't see what good it would do any of us if I told Mr. Hoover all the detailed ways they broke the school rules.

3. The Zora-Amelia fight made me feel pretty icky. I'm glad Zora didn't stand for Amelia making fun of us, but I was tired of her being so mean in the first place.

4. I am sticking with my plan to pretend I don't remember stuff and keep my mouth shut. Those two fights broke out because Zora blabbed that Amelia couldn't ride a bike and Zach blabbed that

Charlie had a crush on Zora. No good can come from speaking up like that. Besides, after all that happened with Mr. Lawrence in Brooklyn, I have learned my lesson about saying too much in principals' offices.

**Three news bulletins on the Mr. Allbright–Nurse Taylor situation**

1. After Charlie and Zach visited Mr. Hoover, they went to Nurse Taylor so she could bandage up their scrapes. Then Nurse Taylor walked them back to the classroom herself. (This is unusual. She usually lets kids make their own way back. Especially fifth graders.)

2. Mr. Allbright gave Zach and Charlie a serious look as they walked to their desks. Then he went and talked to Nurse Taylor for a few minutes. There was lots of smiling. Even some laughing.

3. Everyone else was still staring at Charlie and Zach, but I noticed that Mr. Allbright's face looked a little pink—and that he was still smiling—as he turned away from the door and told us to take out our math workbooks.

**Four unsurprising things Mom said when I got home from school**

1. How was your day?

2. How's your lip?

3. Don't forget to clean out your lunch box.

4. How much homework do you have?

**One surprising thing Mom said when I got home from school**

1. I got a call from Mr. Hoover's secretary today, telling me that it's school policy to let parents know when students are called to the principal's office. And that you had to go see him to talk about an "incident" you witnessed. Do you want to tell me what happened?

My response: Not really? But Mom wasn't having it.

**Nine questions Mom had about my visit to Mr. Hoover**

1. Why did you have to go see him?

2. Why did Zach and Charlie fight?

3. Who threw the first punch?

4. Why was Charlie defending Zora?

5. Why were Zora and Amelia arguing?


(Really, so many questions.)


6. What did Mr. Hoover say when you told him all this?


For about two seconds I debated lying to Mom. It would have been so easy to make something up. But as much as I can pretend to be someone else to the rest of the world—a kid who doesn't notice much, a kid who doesn't remember little details, a kid who just blends in and hangs out—I can't pretend that with Mom. She just knows me too well.

So I took a deep breath, said, "I didn't tell him any of it," and braced myself for the next round of questions:


7. What?! What did you tell him instead?

8. Why didn't you tell the truth?

9. They should be able to count on you to report on things like this. Don't they know what a great memory you have?

### Three things I finally told Mom
-----------------------------------------------------------------

1. No, they don't know what a great memory I have, and I want to keep it that way.

2. I hate my memory. It's embarrassing, and it only gets me into trouble. It got me kicked out of school in Brooklyn.

3. I can never fix the problems my memory caused there, but at least I can keep it under wraps here in Clover Gap.

### Three faces Mom made then
-----------------------------------------------------------------

1. Confused

2. Sad

3. Sadder

### Four confidences Mom laid on me then
-----------------------------------------------------------------

1. You did not do anything wrong in Brooklyn.

2. Dad and I should not have put you in a position where you had to keep our address secret.

3. I have been feeling guilty about that every day.

4. You are like me. You dwell on things that have gone wrong.

And two pieces of Mom wisdom . . .

1. Everyone makes mistakes, including me, as you've learned.

2. You shouldn't hide the person you are from your new friends. You have a lot of funny, wise, and important things to say. And you have a beautiful memory.

**Three helpful tricks Mr. Allbright taught us to make adding fractions easy**

Sorry, I can't report on these because I didn't pay attention. Good luck to you next time you try to add fractions.

**Four things I was actually paying attention to instead**

1. A spider on the ceiling

2. Louis, the kid who sits beside me, drawing a bird

3. The way Mr. Allbright ended almost every sentence with ". . . okay?"

4. Amelia and Zora passing notes whenever Mr. A turned around. Then Zora leaned over to me and whispered that she'd thought of a way to make

her and Amelia get along again. "And you're part of it!" she said, like I should be honored.

## Four things my parents still don't know

1. Every day I throw away the carrot sticks Mom puts in my lunch box.

2. When I'm alone in my room I make faces at myself in the mirror to see how pretty, ugly, scary, or old I can look.

3. When I shoot baskets in our backyard, I quietly sing songs that I make up as I go along.

4. Zora has proposed that she, Kate, Amelia, and I become blood sisters.

## Two reasons Zora wants to be blood sisters

1. She read about it in a book and she thought it sounded cool. (Basically you prick your finger with a pin, and hold your finger against your friends' bloody fingers, and your blood will mix and make you secret sisters.)

2. She's hoping it will make us all get along better.

## Two reasons I predict this will not go well

1. Kate thinks the idea is bonkers and says we can get diseases.

2. Amelia, as I learned during my pencil-lead incident, is terrified of blood.

**Three directions Zora gave in the secret note she passed us about the blood-sisters meeting**

----------------------------------------

1. Meet at Pond Fort today at 3:30.

2. Bring a safety pin. (I'll test everyone's pin and use the sharpest one.)

3. Keep this secret. I'll bring the Band-Aids.

**Three things Zora brought to the blood-sisters ceremony**

----------------------------------------

1. A safety pin

2. A box of Band-Aids

3. A tomato

**Seven things that happened before I shut down the whole production**

1. Zora welcomed us to the blood ceremony and asked us to sit down.

2. At the word "blood," Amelia turned a shade paler.

3. Zora asked us to pass her our safety pins.

4. Amelia's hand was trembling as she passed hers over.

5. Zora opened the first safety pin, drew back her hand, and jammed the point into the tomato as hard as she could.

6. Tomato juice shot out and squirted Amelia in the eye.

7. Amelia screamed, covered her eye, and lay back on the pine needles.


**Two things on my mind at that moment**

1. Blood makes Amelia throw up.

2. Amelia doesn't want anyone to know that blood makes her throw up.


**Four things I did to deflect everyone's attention**

1. Grabbed the tomato from Zora and threw it in the pond.

2. Said, "I thought I saw a worm in that tomato."

3. Put my finger to my lips and said, "Be quiet for a second!"

4. Whispered, "Did you guys hear that? Do you think that was a bear?"

## Three more things that brought the ceremony to a speedy end

1. Amelia said, "Maybe it *was* a bear?"

2. Kate said, "There's no bear. But let's do something else. This is kind of dumb."

3. Zora said, "What the heck did you throw the tomato for, Annie?" And before I could answer, she sighed and added, "I'm going home." Amelia said, "Wait! I'll come with you."

## Two questions Kate asked me after they left

1. Why did you really throw that tomato? (Answer: I didn't think anyone wanted to do the blood-sisters ceremony, and I was trying to get us out of it. I still didn't say anything about Amelia's fear of blood.)

2. Why didn't you just say that sooner? (Answer: I didn't want to make Zora mad.)

Kate admitted that I was right, that Zora was the only one who wanted to do it. "I think we should have told Zora that," she said. I didn't say anything. I thought she might be right, but I didn't know how to do it. And what I'd said was true: I didn't want to make Zora—or anyone—mad. Throwing tomatoes was about as brave as I could be for now.

**Five things I hope I'm brave enough to try someday**

1. Hot-air ballooning

2. Riding a donkey to the bottom of the Grand Canyon

3. Swimming with dolphins

4. Flying a helicopter

5. Traveling to outer space

**Three people I had emails from that night**

1. Grandma Rose, with a collection of cute kitten pictures someone had forwarded her

2. Aunt Pen, with a list of fun things we could do at the beach this summer

3. Kate, with a corny joke about a mama and baby tomato

**One person I did not have an email from that night**

---

1. Millie

She still hadn't responded to my email asking about Charlotte Devlin. Which was pretty much leading me to one conclusion: Charlotte must be her NBF.

**Three answers I gave the next day when Amelia stopped me in the bathroom at school and asked, "Why did you really throw that tomato?"**

---

1. I didn't want to do the blood ceremony.

2. I knew no one else did either.

3. You don't have to admit it, and I still won't tell, but I know blood makes you sick.

**One thing Amelia said then that kind of shocked me**

---

1. Thank you.

**Four things I did later in the day when Zora cornered me on the playground and asked why I threw the tomato**

---

1. Took a deep breath.

2. Said, "I didn't see a worm." (Zora: "I know.")

3. Added, "Or hear a bear." (Zora: "I know.")

4. Blurted out, "I knew no one but you wanted to do the blood-sisters thing. But I think everyone was afraid to tell you they didn't like your idea."

## Four things Zora did in response

1. Narrowed her eyes for just a second.

2. Sighed (again).

3. Said, "You guys should have just said so."

4. Asked if I wanted to go jump rope.

**Five things I thought about for the rest of the day**

-----------------------------------------------------------------

1. I disagreed with someone and she didn't stop being my friend.

2. The person I stood up to was brave and popular . . . and still, she didn't stop being my friend.

3. Amelia seemed to dislike me a little less.

4. You aren't exactly blending in when you speak up the way I did. But what if it's okay not to just blend in all the time?

5. Maybe Mom was right. Maybe I should start trying to use my voice.

# MAY

**Three options I had for last Friday night**

------------------------------------------------------------

1. Stay home and watch a movie with Mom and Dad. (Ted was hanging out with Marcus. He "aced" the audition and got picked as the drummer in Marcus's band; now they practice whenever someone's parents will let them.)

2. Stay home and fall asleep reading a book in my room.

3. Go to a slumber party for Amelia's birthday.

**Three reasons this was a hard choice for me**

------------------------------------------------------------

1. Fear of saying something dumb at Amelia's

2. Distaste for slumber-party games

3. Confusion over being invited to the party because I still wasn't sure how much the hostess liked

me. But maybe—just maybe—she was softening a little after I saved her from the safety-pin bloodbath.

## Three reasons I decided to go to the party anyway

1. Mom and Dad chose *2001: A Space Odyssey* for their Friday night movie. Snoreburger.

2. Zora promised me it would be fun.

3. Zora told me Amelia's house was awesome.

## Seven things I noticed about Amelia's house

1. There are Doritos and sodas in the pantry, and you don't need to ask permission to have them.

2. Amelia has a TV in her room.

3. The bedspread, curtains, and rug in her bedroom all match.

4. Amelia's artwork is all framed.

5. There is a huge oil portrait of Amelia in the living room.

6. There are two stairwells: one from the foyer to the upstairs hallway, and one from the kitchen to Amelia's closet.

7. Amelia's closet is bigger than my bedroom was in Brooklyn.

## Five guests at Amelia's sleepover

1. Me

2. Zora

3. Kate

4. Amelia's neighbor Kya, who's a grade behind us in school

5. Amelia's cousin Hope, age twelve

## Four reasons I found Hope a little intense

1. She was amazingly comfortable around Amelia's parents. I know they are her aunt and uncle, but she talked to them like she was a grown-up too. Like "Aunt Connie, I love your new curtains!" and "Uncle Doug, how is your job?" That sort of thing.

2. As soon as the adults weren't around, she cursed. A lot. "Like a sailor," as my Grandma Elaine would say.

3. When Kya told her she liked her earrings, she said, "Thank you. They're real diamonds."

4. She said Truth or Dare was boring, and that we should just play Dare.

### Twelve things that happened during our game of Dare

1. We pulled names out of a hat to see who would dare whom. ("Whom" again, Mr. A!)

2. I got Kya and dared her to drink a mixture of Sprite, Dr Pepper, and Coke. She did it.

3. Kya got Amelia and dared her to drink a mixture of milk and orange juice. She did.

4. Amelia got Kate and dared her to drink the juice of two lemons. Kate squeezed the lemons into a glass and drank the juice.

5. Kate got Zora and dared her to write something on the bathroom mirror in lipstick. That one would have made me nervous, but Zora just laughed and wrote, "Happy Birthday, Amelia!" in big letters across the whole mirror.

6. Zora got Hope and dared her to stick her hand in a bowl of ice water for two minutes. Hope rolled her eyes and did it.

7. Hope got me.

8. Hope looked at me, tilted her head to the side, and thought for a minute. "I dare you to take something from Doug and Connie's bedroom and bring it downstairs."

9. I thought, *Who the heck are Doug and Connie?* Then I remembered those were Amelia's parents' names.

10. I said, "Do you think you could give me another dare? I don't want to wake them up."

11. "If you're quiet, you won't," Hope answered. "You seem like you're pretty good at being quiet."

12. I waited for someone to back me up on this being a ridiculous idea. No one did.

**Twenty-five things that happened upstairs at Amelia's**

------------------------------------------------------------------

1. I crept into the upstairs hallway as quietly as I could.

2. I saw Amelia's parents' bedroom door at the end of the hallway, waiting for me.

3. About five different scenarios involving scary things hiding behind doors popped into my head.

4. I looked to my left and noticed Amelia's bedroom door standing open.

5. I thought, *Do I really have to go into their bedroom? I bet I can find something that belongs to them in Amelia's room.*

6. I went into Amelia's room and started quietly looking around, thinking that surely Amelia had borrowed *something* from her mom—some makeup, maybe, or a book.

7. I looked on her bookshelf and one title caught my eye. It was *A & Z, Grades K to 3.*

8. I took the book down and saw that it was a photo album. It was filled with pictures of Amelia and Zora from kindergarten to—you guessed it— third grade. The pictures were really cute and smiley. I suddenly missed Millie so much that my stomach hurt.

9. I heard a noise in the doorway. It was Hope. "What are you doing in here?" she hissed. "Your dare was to get something from *their* room," she reminded me as she pointed down the hallway.

10. I quickly put the photo album back on the shelf where I had found it.

11. I tiptoed down the hall to the master bedroom, where the door was open a little.

12. Figuring maybe I didn't have to go the *whole*

way into the room, I slipped my arm inside and started feeling around for something to take.

13. *Crash!* I knocked something over.

14. The smell of roses filled the air.

15. Someone said, "What the—?" and Amelia's dad came running to the door, his eyes bleary.

16. "Annie? Is everything okay?" he asked.

17. "Yes," I said. "Well, I just needed to borrow something from your room."

18. Just then I saw what I had knocked over. It was a bottle of Amelia's mother's perfume, and it was spilling all over the dresser.

19. Amelia's dad asked, "What do you need to borrow?"

20. I quickly righted the perfume bottle and answered, "This. I needed to borrow this."

21. Amelia's dad sighed and said, "Let me guess. Hope put you up to this?"

22. I looked behind me, and Hope had disappeared. I wondered how he knew.

23. "Here," he said, handing me a bottle of lotion instead. "This one won't spill. Will it do?"

24. "Yes," I whispered. "Thank you very much."

25. "Good night, Annie," he said, and he closed the door all the way this time.

I turned and ran down the stairs, thinking that I had just gotten a new most embarrassing moment.

**Four ways Hope took over the rest of the party**

1. She told all of us where we should put our sleeping bags.

2. She made a point of saying Amelia should be near the bathroom "so she doesn't wet the bed." (At this Amelia looked mortified and said, "Hope, I do NOT wet the bed!" Hope just smirked.)

3. She announced that we would play Light as a Feather, and that she would be the person leading the chant every time.

4. She scared us all into staying awake crazy late by saying that the first one to fall asleep would wake up with a Sharpie mustache.

As it turned out, Hope was the first one to fall asleep. She didn't seem very concerned that anyone was going to draw on *her* with Sharpie. And no one did.

**Five things people said about Hope after she fell asleep**

1. Zora: Amelia, why do you let her boss you around so much?

2. Amelia: It's not a big deal. She's my cousin. I like her.

3. Zora: I don't think I'd like her very much if I were you. If someone bossed me around that much, I would say something.

4. Me: It's not always easy to speak up like that, especially when you think someone's scary.

5. Amelia: I'm not scared of her, Annie! Maybe *you* are. You're the one who took that stupid dare from her.


Well, she was right about one thing: I did think Hope was a little scary. Up until then, I had been feeling kind of bad for Amelia. I could see she might have bigger problems than chipped nail polish and hexagonal pencils. But it's hard to keep feeling sympathy for someone who can be so nasty. I was glad when Amelia's mom came downstairs and said, "Lights out, ladies."


**Three things that changed at school after Amelia's slumber party**

1. Kate started calling me Rose because that was the scent of the perfume I spilled.

2. Amelia started making room for me at lunch, and looking at me (instead of just at Zora, Zach, and Charlie) when she told a story.

3. I stopped writing "From A to Z" on my notes to Zora.


After I found that photo album in Amelia's room, it occurred to me that she thought of herself as the original "A" to Zora's "Z." I didn't want her to accuse me of trying to take over.

**Three reasons I didn't email Millie to tell her about the slumber party**

------------------------------------------------------------------------

1. She doesn't know any of the kids here, so it would take a long time to explain everything.

2. Because she doesn't know anyone here, she might not really "get" the stories anyway.

3. She still hasn't emailed me back since she said she was going to the movies with Juliette and Charlotte.

**Four possible reasons Millie has not emailed me since then**

------------------------------------------------------------------------

1. Maybe while she was at the movies, someone broke into her apartment and stole her family's computer.

2. Maybe the movie-theater floor was so dirty that her feet are still stuck to it.

3. Maybe the theater was actually a secret portal to Narnia.

4. Maybe Millie is best friends with Juliette and Charlotte now, and she doesn't need me anymore.


**One new word I learned the day after the slumber party**
------------------------------------------------------------------------------
1. Kerning


After I had put away my pillow and my sleeping bag, I grabbed a snack and started doing my hovering bit with Mom while she worked in her office. (She almost never used to work on Saturdays, but now she says, "Who am I to turn down an extra assignment?") Mom was fiddling with a word on her computer screen for a really long time. She would click on it, press some buttons, click on it again, press more buttons, and on and on. Every time she pressed buttons, the spaces between the characters would change just a tiny bit, making the letters either closer together or farther apart. I asked Mom what she was doing, and she said, "It's called kerning. I'm making it so that the letters aren't too close or too far apart. So that the word will look just right."

**One weird dream I had that night**

1. A bunch of kids I knew—Zora, Kate, Amelia, Zach, Charlie, Ted, Marcus, Millie, Charlotte, and even the mysterious Juliette—were standing in a line. I was right in the middle. And we kept scooching closer together, then farther apart. Closer together, then farther apart. We were kerning, trying to get the spacing just right.

**Five things I have heard about way more in Clover Gap than I ever did in Brooklyn**

1. Bicycles

2. Kickball

3. Deer droppings

4. Clovers

5. Trees

**Eight things people here discuss about trees**

1. How old they are

2. How big they are

3. Whether they have carpenter ants

4. Whether they have a tree disease

5. Whether they might fall in a storm

6. Which direction they would fall if they were to fall in a storm

7. Which "tree guy" to use to take care of them. (When the weather started warming up, Mom said, "We have to find a tree guy." Ted and I asked, "Why do we need a tree guy?" Mom promised us we'd see soon enough. Surprisingly, Dad didn't say anything about money or offer to check the trees himself. I think his near fall from the roof humbled him a little.)

8. What kind of animals might be living in the tree

For us, the answer to that last one was: raccoons.

**Four animals that scare me**

----------------------------------------------------------------

1. Bears (of course)

2. Snakes

3. Wasps

4. Lice

**Four things the tree guy said when he came to check our giant oak tree**

---

1. The top half of that tree is hollow.

2. I could fit almost my whole body into it.

3. There's a family of raccoons living in there.

4. We have to take it down.

The tree guy explained that the tree was weak because it was hollow, and if they didn't take it down the safe way, it could come down the dangerous way (like falling on our house during a storm). So he brought out a crew and they climbed the tree and cut it down bit by bit, using ropes to lower each section to the ground. It was pretty amazing to watch. But now the raccoons were homeless.

**Three crazy things I've seen in the backyard since we moved here**

---

1. A squirrel fight

2. Flying turkeys (Who knew?!)

3. A coyote (Ted didn't see it and says it had to have been a dog; I know what I saw.)

**Three homes the raccoon mama tried out after the tree came down**

1. Our garbage cans (until Mom and Dad found a way to lock them closed)

2. The woodpile beside the porch (but this wasn't very private)

3. Our basement window well

The window well is the one she settled on. There is a long wooden bench covering the window well that protects it from the rain (but left just enough of an opening for her to squeeze through with her babies, one by one).

**Three things we learned after Dad called animal control and got connected to the town "raccoon lady"**

1. Don't go near the raccoons, because their mama is very protective and she will try to attack you.

2. A raccoon with that many babies (six!) is probably an older mother. ("Poor thing," Mom said under her breath.)

3. The animal-control people will not move baby raccoons. If you wait a couple of weeks, the mama will take them out on her own.

This started the phenomenon that came to be known in our house as the raccoon aquarium (and of course Ted thought that should be a band name).

**Six amazing things about the raccoon aquarium**

1. We could stand on the old sofa in our basement and watch the raccoons through the window whenever we wanted.

2. There were six baby raccoons. (We learned that they're called "kits.")

3. We got to watch them play.

4. We got to watch them nurse.

5. We sort of became neighborhood celebrities, because everyone wanted to come see the raccoons.

6. Dad couldn't get enough of them.

**Five ways we could tell that the raccoons were helping Dad warm up to Clover Gap**

1. He would stand on the sofa and watch them longer than anyone else.

2. The first thing he did every day when he got home from work was check on the kits.

3. He took about a hundred pictures of them.

4. He also checked on them every night before he went to bed, and he would give Mom updates. (I think he felt extra protective of the kits at night, because that was when the mama raccoon left them to look for food.)

5. He kept saying, "This never happened in Brooklyn!" (The third time he said that, I noticed Mom giving Ted a look to see what his reaction was. But he didn't really have one. I think Clover Gap was starting to grow on him, too.)

The raccoon family left after about two weeks, just like the raccoon lady said they would. The mama moved the babies out one by one, and Dad didn't leave the basement until they were all gone (he was especially worried about the last one, which sat in the window well all alone and mewled like a kitten until the mama returned).

Late that night, I woke up to go to the bathroom, and I had to wait in the hall while Mom and Dad finished brushing their teeth. I heard them talking about the raccoons. "They seemed so cozy there," Dad said. "It was their home. How do they even know where they're supposed to go next?"

"They needed room to grow," Mom said. "I think they'll figure it out. And eventually they'll be cozy in their new home too, don't you think? I mean, we know a little something about that." Mom caught Dad's eye in the bathroom mirror. He stopped flossing for a second and smiled at her.

"Yeah," he said. "I guess we do."

Dad was a little mopey the next day, but pretty soon he started getting excited about other signs of spring in Clover Gap. Like the baby deer we sometimes saw in the backyard, and the wild turkeys. And, of course, the clovers.

# JUNE

## Three things that happen in Clover Gap in June

1. People start cooking outside a lot.

2. Flowers I never heard of before pop up everywhere (peonies, freesias, and bleeding hearts, which are little, purplish pink, and actually shaped like hearts).

3. Clover Fest (Apparently, this matters more than all the rest. In June, Clover Gap goes crazy for clovers.)

## Three questions I asked Zora about Clover Fest

1. Why is it such a big deal? (Answer: It's like the most fun time of the whole year here. Better than Halloween.)

2. What do you do there? (There are carnival rides. And a petting zoo with farm animals. And a

209

four-leaf clover hunt. And a beauty pageant where they crown a Miss Clover and a Junior Miss Clover. And everyone makes recipes using clovers, and there's a contest to see whose is the best.)

3. Isn't it weird that it's in June? I mean, since Saint Patrick's Day is in March? (Answer, accompanied by a blank stare: What are you talking about? Saint Patrick's Day is for shamrocks. Clovers are completely different.)

### One question I asked Kate about Clover Fest

1. Is it really as awesome as Zora says it is? (Answer: Yes! Clover Fest is the best.)

Since Kate is usually more subdued than Zora, I'm starting to believe the hype.

### Two things about Clover Fest I'm looking forward to

1. Rides

2. Petting zoo

### Three things about Clover Fest that just sound weird

1. Clover recipes

2. Miss Clover pageant

3. Junior Miss Clover pageant

**Three ways my family is being surprisingly enthusiastic about Clover Fest**

------------------------------------------------------------

1. Mom is searching the local consignment store for clover-themed clothing we can all wear. (Ted and I keep saying no thanks to that one.)

2. Ted says the band got a "sweet gig" playing after the pageant. And they have finally decided on a name for themselves: Mind the Gap. (Ted explained to the other guys that in some cities, subway doors have signs on them telling people to "mind the gap" so they won't accidentally step into the space between the platform and the train. And since the name of our town is Clover *Gap*, well . . . The guys thought it was genius. I've never seen Ted look so proud.)

3. Dad is making time to experiment with clover recipes. Clover salad, clover pesto, clover cookies. It's good to see Dad getting back in his groove in the kitchen, but still . . . clover cookies?

At least I'm hoping this will be an end to Mom, Ted, and me being in charge of dinners, which have been mostly a rotation of burgers: hamburgers, turkey burgers, veggie burgers . . . snoreburger.

**Four things the kids at school are planning for Clover Fest**

---

1. Zach's dad is a farmer, and he's going to loan one of his sheep to the petting zoo.

2. Zora is going on the Tilt-a-Whirl for the first time. (She said her parents put an age minimum on it after Marcus went on it and barfed when he was eight.)

3. Kate is ironing clover patches onto her favorite jeans.

4. Amelia's cousin Hope is in the running for Junior Miss Clover, and she told Amelia she could help her get ready backstage.


**Three questions I asked Mom, who grew up going to her county fair in North Carolina**

---

1. Is it like a street fair in Brooklyn? (Answer: Not really. There's a lot of good food like there is at street fairs. But there are also rides. It's more like Coney Island with farm animals.)

2. Will it be like the fair in *Charlotte's Web*? (Answer: I guess? My county fairs were. But apparently this one will also have lots of clovers.)

3. Am I allowed to hang out with my friends on my own, or do I have to stay with you the whole time? (Answer: You can hang out with your friends as

long as you stay with them. And you have to do a check-in with me at a certain time.)

I pointed out that if I had my own cell phone, I could just text her and we wouldn't have to arrange a check-in. She smiled and said it wasn't a big deal; she was okay with the check-in. No big surprise there.

**First five thoughts that popped into my head when I got to Clover Fest**

1. I had no idea there were this many people in Clover Gap.

2. There's a Ferris wheel, and it looks pretty high.

3. Even though there's so much people noise— laughing, shouting to friends, babies crying—it's almost drowned out by the carnival music.

4. The smell is as strong as the music. Depending on which way the wind blows, the fairgrounds either smell like funnel cake, candy apples, hot dogs, or pizza . . . *or* cows, sheep, and pigs. Or sometimes all those smells at the same time.

5. I see Kate and Zora!

They were waiting for me by the ticket booth. "Come on," said Zora. "Let's see if we can rescue Amelia from pageant land."

**Four things Mom made me promise before she let me leave with them**

------------------------------------------------------------

1. I would not leave "the group."

2. I would not talk to strangers.

3. If I got lost or separated from the group, I would ask another mom for help.

4. I would meet her at the pageant stage in an hour.

**Three things that prevented me from meeting Mom an hour later**

------------------------------------------------------------

1. Amelia throwing up on the Tilt-a-Whirl

2. Amelia's throw-up landing on Zora and Kate

3. Me, by default, having to pinch-hit as Hope's pageant helper

**Three reasons I should have known Amelia might get sick on the Tilt-a-Whirl**

------------------------------------------------------------

1. She ate almost an entire funnel cake before we got on.

2. She started looking a little green before the ride even started.

3. As you know, I had witnessed Amelia's sensitive puke reflex in the past.

But I gave her the benefit of the doubt this time. I knew she wanted it to be a secret. Besides, I figured no blood was involved, so maybe she was safe. I was wrong.

**Four places Amelia's funnel cake landed after it came back up**

---

1. Amelia's shirt

2. The seat of the Tilt-a-Whirl car

3. Zora's shoes

4. Kate's jeans

Somehow the vomit missed me. Zora and Kate said they were going to have to take Amelia somewhere and clean themselves up. I thought I was lucky, until Amelia said, "Annie, since you're the only one with no sick on you, will you go tell Hope that I can't help her get ready for the pageant?"

**Two things I said to try to get out of this assignment**

---

1. I told my mom I'd stay with you guys. (Amelia said it was okay because her mom and her aunt would be with Hope too.)

2. I have to meet my parents at seven o'clock. (Amelia's response: That's right when the pageant starts, so you'll be fine.)

**One way I could tell Hope had no idea who I was when I showed up backstage at the pageant**

---

1. When I found her in the dressing room for contestants, wearing a shimmery green leotard and looking at herself in the mirror as she put on green eye makeup, she said, "Who are you?"

**Four things I said to identify myself, waiting for Hope's blank stare to go away**

---

1. I'm Annie.

2. I'm Amelia's friend.

3. I was at her slumber party.

4. I'm the one who spilled the perfume.

Finally that one seemed to register.

**Three questions everyone had next**
-----------------------------------------

1. Hope: Why are you here?

2. Hope's mom: Sorry—who are you, dear?

3. Amelia's mom: Where's Amelia?


Here I was torn. I figured Amelia wouldn't care if her mom knew about her throwing up, but I was guessing she wouldn't want Hope to know. So I said the first thing that popped into my head: "She spilled her drink on herself, and she had to get cleaned up. Zora and Kate are with her." At this news Hope rolled her eyes, turned back toward the mirror, and said, "What is it with you kids and spills?"


**One alarming order I was given next**
-----------------------------------------

1. From Hope's mom: Well, we still need another set of hands. If it's only you here, you'll have to help us.


**Three reasons I was the worst possible person to help Hope get ready for the pageant**
-----------------------------------------

1. I knew nothing about pageants.

2. I knew nothing about the things that seemed very important in pageants: Makeup. Fancy dresses. Perfect hair. Public speaking.

3. I was not exactly a fan of Hope.

### Three pageant-assistant assignments I was given

1. Hold Hope's hair in a tight bun while the moms pin clover barrettes around it. (Yes, apparently this is a three-person job.)

2. Shield Hope's costume with a sheet while the moms spritz her face lightly with green glitter (again, three people on this task).

3. Guard Hope's backup baton. Why did she have a backup baton, you ask? Well, in case something happened to her first baton, of course. (Hope's act for the talent portion of the pageant was a baton-twirling routine.)

### My new most embarrassing moment

1. Walking onstage in the middle of the Junior Miss Clover pageant to retrieve the backup baton, which I accidentally tossed from backstage during Hope's performance

### Two things that Amelia and Hope had apparently worked out during their pre-pageant practice

1. The steps of Hope's baton routine, including one part where she puts down the baton, looks to the side, and does a little wave

2. An emergency signal that would let Amelia know Hope needed the backup baton

**Two things Hope forgot to tell me because she was so nervous**

------------------------------------------------------------

1. The steps of the routine (the side wave part would have been particularly good to know)

2. The emergency signal

So that is why, when Hope dropped her baton, looked offstage, and waved, I was not aware that it was meant to be a "fun and whimsical" gesture (as she would later tell me). I assumed she had determined her first baton was defective and was motioning for me to toss her the new one.

**Two clues that immediately told me I was not supposed to have tossed the baton**

------------------------------------------------------------

1. The horrified look on Hope's face

2. The gasp from Hope's mother, who was standing behind me in the wings

Hope froze as her music continued and the baton rolled merrily toward the front of the stage, coming to a stop right at the edge. And then it was my turn to be horrified, because Hope's mother nudged me and hissed, "You have to go get it!"

### Three ways it was clear I did not belong on that stage

1. I was not sporting a single clover. (My observance of the dress code included jeans and a green T-shirt.)

2. My hair was in a ponytail (and not styled, sprayed, and sparkly, like the hair of the contestants).

3. I couldn't even hold on to a baton, much less twirl and catch it.

### Four things I could see from the stage

1. My parents and Zora's parents gaping at me from our designated meeting spot

2. Ted and Marcus and their bandmates staring, openmouthed

3. Also staring: Zach, Charlie, Charlie's mom, and Charlie's grandmother

4. Zora, Amelia, and Kate, cleaned up and dressed in head-to-toe Clover Fest gear

**Six people who started laughing**

---

1. Ted

2. Marcus

3. Charlie

4. Zach

5. Zora

6. Kate

**Four people who were definitely NOT laughing**

---

1. Charlie's grandma

2. Hope

3. Hope's mother

4. Amelia

**Two things Hope's mother hissed from backstage**

---

1. Get off that stage! (to me)

2. Just keep going! (to Hope)

So Hope kept going. I have to give her some credit; she seemed to make it through the rest of the routine pretty smoothly (although I can't say for sure that she didn't make any mistakes, since I hadn't watched her practice a hundred times like Amelia had).

And I got off the stage as fast as I could. I handed the backup baton to Hope's mom, whispered, "I'm so sorry," and ran out into the crowd to find my parents.

### Five things people said when I got out into the audience

1. Dad: Hey, you're famous!

2. Ted: Nice one, Annie. You literally dropped the baton.

3. Kate: That was kind of amazing.

4. Amelia: Hope's going to kill me. And now I have to help her get ready for the evening gown competition. (She was really pale, like she might get sick again. Without saying goodbye to anyone, she bolted for the dressing room.)

5. Mom: Honey, are you okay?

Was I okay? I wasn't so sure. Hope was a pretty awful person; I didn't much care that I'd messed up her routine. But I knew Amelia was afraid of her, and now she was going to have to pay for my mistake.

### Three pageant titles that Hope did not win

1. Junior Miss Clover

2. Most Talented

3. Miss Congeniality

**One pageant title that Hope did win**

---

1. Miss Photogenic

Amelia had told us that Hope was predicting from the beginning that she would get that one, because she claimed it went to the prettiest girl in the pageant. But I knew it wouldn't be enough to make her forget the baton blunder.

**The three scariest parts of Clover Fest**

---

1. The Crazy Clover Roller Coaster (according to Ted and Marcus, though I had to take their word for it because I was too short to ride it)

2. The operator of the Tilt-a-Whirl, who was rumored to be an escaped convict (Mom said that was ridiculous, though she didn't sound positive.)

3. The sight of Miss Photogenic Clover, moments after the pageant ended, lunging toward me with murder in her eyes

**Four things Hope accused me of**

---

1. Being a gigantic klutz

2. Being a moron

3. Destroying her baton routine

4. Losing her the Junior Miss Clover title

**Five people who started to jump to my defense**

1. Mom

2. Dad

3. Ted

4. Kate

5. Zora

**One person who interrupted them and put Hope in her place**

1. Me

I did. I looked big bad Hope straight in the eye and said, "I'm sorry your baton routine got messed up. But I did the best I could. And you are so terrible to people all the time that I'm pretty sure you lost the pageant all by yourself."

**Three awesome things that happened then**

1. The crowd erupted into cheers.

2. My friends lifted me onto their shoulders.

3. Hope tore her Miss Photogenic sash into shreds and ran from the fairgrounds.

Just kidding. A girl can dream. It was more like this:

**Three things that happened after I stood up to Hope**

1. Hope stared at me for a second, then turned and left with her mom.

2. My mom gave me a quick shoulder squeeze and whispered, "Nice going, kid."

3. Kate looped her arm through mine and asked if I was allowed to go with her and Zora for cotton candy before the band played.


Zora asked Amelia if she was going to join us, but she shook her head. "I think I'm done with Clover Fest for today," she said, then turned and left with her mom. I couldn't tell if she was mad at me or not. I had a feeling that as nasty as Hope had been to me, she had probably lit into Amelia even more when she'd gone backstage. And Amelia still had to be her cousin.

When we returned to our parents and the area by the pageant stage with our cotton candy, there was still a crowd waiting to hear the band. I was glad Ted and Marcus were going to have a big audience, but I also felt a little nervous for them. Most of their practices I'd overheard had sounded pretty rusty.


**Twelve things I heard in the first few minutes of Ted and Marcus's band performance**

1. High-pitched feedback sounds as Marcus tried to adjust his guitar amp

2. A low electric hum before Ted started his drum line

3. The bass player, Lee, strumming a chord

4. Marcus's voice singing the beginning of their opening song (He was a little hard to hear at first, but with each word his voice got stronger. I had to admit, they weren't doing too badly. In fact, their band actually sounded, well, *good*.)

5. Charlie's grandma saying, "We don't need to hear this racket. Let's go to the bake sale."

6. Charlie's response: "Grandma, my friends' brothers are in this band. I want to stay."

7. Charlie's grandma again, as she frowned and squinted at the stage: "Which ones are your friends' brothers?"

8. An interruption from Charlie's mom: "Mother, why don't you go ahead to the bake sale on your own. I'll stay here with Charlie."

9. "Fine," Charlie's grandma snipped as she turned to leave. "But I don't know how you can listen to this."

10. Zora's mom quietly stepping up beside us and saying, "Hey, Lisa," to Charlie's mom.

11. Charlie's mom saying, "Hey, Rhonda," with a small smile. "The band sounds great."

12. Zora cutting in with "Mom, can we go up front? Marcus said Ted might throw his drumsticks into the crowd at the end."

I didn't care about catching a drumstick, considering they were all over the place at my house. But I was still glad when the moms said okay (including my mom, who gave my shoulder another little squeeze). Charlie was happy too; the miserable look on his face totally disappeared when Zora grabbed his arm and said, "Let's go!"

As I worked my way through the crowd with my friends, I wondered how much Zora's mom had heard Charlie's grandma complaining about the band. I wondered what Zora's mom and Charlie's mom would talk about after we left. I wondered how much things had changed for the two of them since they were kids growing up together.

I turned around and looked at them after we got to the front of the crowd, and they were both standing quietly, listening to the boys play. No one in our group caught a drumstick, but I did see Marcus toss Charlie a guitar pick.

**One part of Clover Fest where no one is allowed until the last day**

- - - - - - - - - - - - - - - - - - - - - - - - - - - - - - - - - - - - - - - - - - - - - - - - - - - - -

1. The Four-Leaf Clover Field

Every day while the rest of the fairgrounds are swarming with people, one field is roped off (with green ribbon, of course), and no one is allowed to walk there. I asked Kate why we couldn't go in and she said, "That's the Four-Leaf Clover Field. You can't go there until the last day, when they let all the kids in to look for a four-leaf clover."

**Three things you are guaranteed to find in the Four-Leaf Clover Field**

---

1. Grass

2. Dirt

3. Millions and millions of three-leaf clovers

**One thing you are NOT guaranteed to find in the Four-Leaf Clover Field**

---

1. A four-leaf clover

"What?!" Ted said when Marcus told him that. "They don't even sneak in a four-leaf clover from somewhere else to make sure someone finds one?"

Marcus seemed surprised in the way that all Clover Gappers (or is it Clover Gapites? Gapians? Gapsters? Gaplanders?) get when any outsiders express confusion about Clover Fest. "No," he explained, speaking slowly to Ted. "That would be cheating. Some years nobody finds one. But if you *do* find one, you're considered the Luckiest Kid in Clover Gap for a whole year."

Ted thought this was the stupidest thing he'd ever heard, not that it mattered, because he couldn't be in the four-leaf clover hunt anyway. (It's only for kids eleven and under.)

But Mom seemed to think it was charming, and Dad thought it was the coolest thing ever. With the news about the four-leaf clover hunt that might actually never turn up a four-leaf clover, it seemed that Dad's conversion to Clover Gapper (I'm going with "Gapper") was complete. It was also clear that I had no choice but to participate; Dad was just too excited.

**Three things I want to teach kids in Clover Gap, now that I am finding my voice here**

1. How to play wall ball

2. All the words to "Parents Just Don't Understand" and "It's the End of the World As We Know It" (These are old songs Millie's dad knows; he helped us memorize the words when we were bored one day after school.)

3. What an urban legend is

I decided to tackle the last one first. Because everyone here seems a little crazypants over the four-leaf clover business.

**Four stories about the four-leaf clover hunt that people in town believe to be 100 percent true**

1. One year, the kid who found the four-leaf clover got kicked by a horse in the petting zoo later that day, and it didn't even give her a bruise.

2. Another year, the four-leaf clover finder went on to become the winner of the town spelling bee.

3. One magical year, the winning kid found a *five*-leaf clover, which is supposed to bring luck *and* money, and the next day, her family won a five-hundred-dollar raffle.

4. No one has ever found a six-leaf clover, but if that ever happens, get excited, because "everyone" knows that six-leaf clovers bring fame.


**Three things I tried to explain about urban legends**

1. The fact that no one is quite able to recall the names of these lottery-winning, phenomenal-spelling, horse-kick-surviving clover finders makes these stories suspicious.

2. One surefire sign that a story is an urban legend is that no one can remember who it happened to, or everyone says it happened to "my cousin's friend" or "my neighbor's aunt" or something like that.

3. Urban legends are just that—*legends*. Stories that

are made up, but that people believe to be true. Besides, who ever heard of a six-leaf clover?

**People who took my reasoning to heart**
-------------------------------------------------------------------
1.



No one. No one seemed to care for my logical explanations. Not even Kate the skeptic. Oh well. Even though my friends didn't listen, I was glad I had tried. (Turns out speaking up gets easier the more you do it.)

**Two reasons I decided to go ahead with the clover hunt despite my doubts**
-------------------------------------------------------------------
1. If you are under twelve years old in Clover Gap on the last day of Clover Fest, there is literally nothing to do other than join the hunt for a four-leaf clover.

2. I have to admit I'm a little curious.

**Three instructions we were given before the start of the clover hunt**
-------------------------------------------------------------------
1. Do your best to walk *around* the clovers, not on them.

2. Please stay at least three feet away from all other clover hunters.

3. If you find a four-leaf clover, pick it carefully, raise it above your head, and yell, "Four!" A clover judge will come over to verify your finding. (At this point I saw Dad looking enviously at the clover judges with their green badges. I knew he was wondering how he could get that job next year.)

### One item each kid got before the hunt started

1. A plastic magnifying glass. (That's another rule: "Only these standard-issue magnifying glasses will be permitted. Any magnifying glasses that are smuggled into the hunt will be confiscated!" Yikes.)

### Three kids who seem to have an edge in the hunt (and the weird things I remember about them that make me think this)

1. Eric Newland (I overheard him bragging to another kid about his better-than-20/20 vision on the day the school nurse checked our vision. In September.)

2. Bonnie Diaz (She is a word-hunt queen. On snowy days, when we had to have recess inside, the lunch aides would keep us busy with things like crossword puzzles and word hunts, and Bonnie always, always finished her word hunts

in no time. And I figure that hunting for four-leaf clovers is kind of like hunting for hidden words.)

3. Bridget Rooney (As much as people here try to distance Clover Fest from Saint Patrick's Day and Irish stuff, I don't think Bridget is having it. She is very, *very* into being Irish-American, and yesterday in the Tilt-a-Whirl line, I heard her saying to some other girls, "I must make my ancestors proud. That four-leaf clover is MINE!" Yikes again.)

**Three kids who likely don't have a prayer of winning**

1. Clark Middleton (He has terrible seasonal allergies. I don't know the kid, but I have noticed him having sneezing attacks outside school every day since mid-March. I can't imagine it's easy to focus on a patch of clovers when you can't stop sneezing. Frankly, I was surprised his parents even let him participate, but I guess one thing I've learned is that Clover Gap takes the four-leaf clover hunt *very* seriously.)

2. Amelia (The clover field is kind of muddy, and from what everyone has told me, you have to spend a lot of time on your knees if you want to have a chance of finding a four-leafer. It may not surprise you to hear that Amelia is not one to willingly get her clothes dirty. So I can't see her going all-out in the hunt. Of course, as crazy

as everyone gets during Clover Fest, you never know.)

3. Me (Rookie disadvantage. I've never participated in the hunt, nor have I even looked for a four-leaf clover anywhere else. I think it's also fair to say that my level of interest and motivation is considerably lower than that of my opponents.)

## Three rituals that preceded the beginning of the clover hunt

1. Singing of the national anthem by the Clover Chorus

2. Recitation of a brief history of Clover Fest by the mayor

3. Cutting of the ribbon that roped off the entrance to the clover field, accompanied by the charge to "Find that four-leaf clover!" (this from the president of the Clover Council)

And with that, the loudspeakers started blaring, "I'm Looking Over a Four-Leaf Clover," and we kids were released into the great green hunting ground.

**Four hunting strategies employed by my friends after the ribbon was cut**

1. Charlie and Zora: Run at top speed to the opposite side of the field to claim the spots that are farthest from the crowd.

2. Zach: Drop to the ground and start walking on your knees while surveying the ground with the magnifying glass.

3. Amelia: Seek out a shady spot to the side, fold a monogrammed beach towel, and sit on it while peering carefully at the clovers.

4. Kate: Wait for the crowd to disperse, then patiently sort through a trampled spot near the entrance.


And me? As usual, I was pretty distracted by people. There was way too much to watch for me to be able to focus on the ground.

**A few things I noticed as the other kids were scrambling in the field**

1. Eric Newland standing straight and tall while examining a spot in the middle of the field (I guess when you have better-than-20/20 vision, you don't have to bend over to find a four-leaf clover.)

2. Bridget Rooney bending over the field like a giant bug, her face centimeters away from the ground as the shamrock antennas on her headband bobbed every time she moved

3. Bonnie Diaz unnerving the other kids each time she picked a clover and examined it closely

4. Poor Clark Middleton sneezing on his magnifying glass and wiping it clean

5. Mr. Allbright and Nurse Taylor standing together on the sidelines, laughing and drinking clover shakes

6. Mom chatting with Kate's mom and taking pictures of the whole scene

7. Dad signing a clipboard at the Clover Council table

8. Ted throwing a Frisbee to Marcus. A Frisbee that he threw a bit too hard, so that Marcus missed it and it flew over the heads of the crowd and beyond the ribbon around the clover field, until it came to a stop about two feet from where I was standing.

**Two things I did not see when I bent down to pick up the Frisbee**

1. A four-leaf clover

2. A five-leaf clover

**Two things I did see when I bent down to pick up the Frisbee**

1. A bunch of three-leaf clovers

2. One six-leaf clover

**Four things I heard after picking up the six-leafer to examine it**

1. At first nothing but my own inner voice, counting to be sure: *One, two, three, four, five, six. One, two, three, four, five, six.*

2. Ted yelling, "Annie, what are you doing? Throw back the Frisbee!"

3. My dad saying, "I think she found something."

4. The mayor and the president of the Clover Council saying, "Young lady, what's going on? Do you have something there?"

**One moment of my life I actually have a hard time remembering clearly**

1. This one. The moment that I became the first kid ever to find a six-leaf clover in the Clover Fest clover hunt.

**Seven things I do remember**

1. The ten members of the Clover Council sprinting over to confirm my discovery

2. Being led to a platform, where the mayor made some kind of announcement about my finding the first-ever six-leaf clover in Clover Gap, and how this would make me and the town famous

3. My dad beaming

4. My mom keeping a hand on my shoulder the whole time

5. Ted yelling, "That's my sister!"

6. Lots of people taking pictures

7. The Clover Council president taking the clover and promising to return it to me once it had been "properly preserved"

**Four reasons the rest is so hard to recall**

1. It happened very fast.

2. It was really noisy.

3. There were too many people around for me to notice much about any of them.

4. I couldn't stop thinking.

**Four things I was thinking**
------------------------------------------------------------

1. This is so crazy.

2. This is kind of fun.

3. This is also a little scary.

4. So much for blending into the background.

**One person who interrupted my swirling thoughts**
------------------------------------------------------------

1. Amelia

**Three things Amelia said that could have knocked me over with a feather. (Mom says that sometimes. It means something's really surprising.)**
------------------------------------------------------------

1. Congratulations.

2. In my family, you're already famous for the way you stood up to Hope last night. No one has ever done that before.

3. Thanks for not telling her that I threw up.

"But maybe I should have," I said. "Then she would have been more understanding."

**Seven more things Amelia said after she stopped laughing**

1. Hope never understands anyone's problems but her own.

2. She was furious at me last night.

3. Sorry I left early, but I didn't want to be at Clover Fest any more.

4. I was upset on the way home, but my mom gave me a good pep talk and told me Hope needs to get over herself.

5. I think that messed-up routine was the worst thing that's ever happened to her.

6. I have to see if I can get a video of it.

7. Want to go get some clover shakes with Zora and me?

And then I felt like we had turned a corner. Amelia inviting me to do something with just her and Zora . . . that had definitely never happened before.

**Three things I decided not to bring up as we walked to meet Zora at the shake stand**

---

1. The times Amelia had been weird to me throughout the school year (She was trying; I had to give her credit for that. Let bygones be bygones, my dad would say.)

2. The *A & Z* photo album I saw in her room (It was obvious by now that Kate's hunch was right: Amelia had been chilly to me because she and Zora had always been tight, and she was having a hard time letting me inside the circle. I know how I would have felt if some new kid had moved to Brooklyn and suddenly become great friends with Millie while I was still there. I mean, look what happened when Millie made new friends after I was gone.)

3. The fact that I don't really like clover shakes (With all the good vibes in the air, it just didn't seem like the time to point out that they have a bitter aftertaste. Not surprisingly, people here love their clover shakes.)


**Five remarks made by my family on the way home from the clover hunt**

---

1. Dad: Wasn't this an amazing day? Isn't this an amazing little town?

2. Ted: The fame thing is kind of self-fulfilling, isn't

241

it? I mean, of course a six-leaf clover will bring you fame, because it's so rare that everyone winds up hearing about it. It's not like there's any magic involved. (I had to admit he had a point.)

3. Mom: Are you all right, Annie? You're awfully quiet.

4. Me: I'm okay. I'm always quiet!

5. Ted: Not really. Not anymore.

Mom turned around and smiled. She knew Ted was right; I wasn't so quiet anymore. But I didn't have many words just then. It had been a crazy day. And it was about to get crazier.

**Three kinds of people I half expected to see at my house when we returned**

---

1. A news crew

2. A marching band

3. A crowd of photographers

**One person I did NOT expect to see at my house when we returned**

---

1. Millie

But there she was, sitting on our front steps, holding a wrapped package. Her mom and dad were standing in the yard, checking out the rosebushes.

**First words spoken by each grown-up**

---

1. Dad: Hey, strangers!

2. Mom: You guys!

3. Millie's dad: Hey, yourself!

4. Millie's mom: Annie, we hear you're famous!

At which point I thought, *Whoa, maybe it is true about the six-leaf clover bringing you fame.* Because how else would they know already?

**Two things Ted said to bring me back to reality**

1. Dad, you posted about the clover on Facebook, didn't you? (Oh yeah, that would explain how they knew.)

2. Annie, aren't you going to talk?

**Five things I had been wanting to say to Millie for months**

1. Why haven't you written to me?

2. Why didn't you answer my question about Charlotte?

3. What's going on back in Brooklyn?

4. Are you still my friend?

5. Will I ever see you again?

At least now I had an answer to that last one.

**The only thing I could think to say to Millie at that moment**

1. Why are you here?

Millie was quiet. After a heavy few seconds, her dad explained that our house was on the way to some relatives they were visiting, so they thought they'd stop in and surprise us.

I was definitely surprised.

**How Millie finally broke her silence**

--------------------------------------------------------------------

1. Hi, Annie.

2. Can I see inside your house?

**Things I said as I gave Millie a tour of the house**

--------------------------------------------------------------------

1. This is the living room.

2. This is the dining room.

3. This is the kitchen.

4. Those are the basement stairs.

5. Out there is the backyard.

6. Upstairs are the bedrooms and bathrooms.

You get the picture. I was barely speaking to her. I was being terse, to use a Mr. Allbright word.

**Why was I being terse?**

--------------------------------------------------------------------

1. I was thinking about the unanswered email.

2. I was wondering if she was best friends with Charlotte now.

3. I was wondering how she could ask for a tour of my house without explaining any of that stuff first.

**Two things Millie and I said at the exact same time:**

---

1. Millie: Can I see your room?

2. Me: How come you stopped writing back to me?

I repeated my question: "Why did you stop writing back to me?"

**Reasons Millie gave for not writing**

---

1. I didn't know what to say.

2. I knew you'd be mad if I told you that you were right—that it was Charlotte Devlin I was going to the movies with. I didn't know how to tell you that she's actually a lot nicer now. I think it has something to do with her getting braces?

When I told Millie she was getting off topic, she looked surprised that I had interrupted her. But she said okay and continued. . . .

3. You sounded like you had a bunch of new friends here, and it made me feel weird.

Finally she said, "You're right, though. I should have written. I'm sorry. Can I show you what I brought?"

**Three things I thought might have been in the wrapped box Millie brought**

---

1. Brooklyn bagels

2. A friendship bracelet

3. My *Guinness Book of World Records*, which she had borrowed and never gave back

**Two things that were in the box**

---

1. A hand turkey with the words "Happy VERY Belated Thanksgiving" written on it

2. A marble notebook, the one we had started writing notes to each other in right before I found out I was moving.

"Open it," Millie said.

**Fifty-one notes that were in the marble notebook**

---

1. On the first page, the last note I wrote to Millie in Brooklyn. It just said, "I think I blabbed to Mr. Lawrence about something I shouldn't have. I'll tell you more about it at lunch."

2–51. Notes Millie wrote to me during all the months I was gone.

"There's not much in it for the months when I was good about emailing," she said when she saw my surprised face. "Then, for a while after you asked about Charlotte, I started feeling weird about not writing you back, and I wasn't sure what to say. But I kept the notes going all along, see?" She flipped through the pages and I could see, in her funny, pointy handwriting, reports on everything that had happened to her in Brooklyn that year. I knew I would take time to read all of them later, but for now certain things jumped out at me: the names of kids in our class, a goofy cartoon of Mr. Lawrence, doodles of stars and planets, and a few times—in big letters—the words "SORRY" and "ARGH! I wish you were here!"

I haven't been much of a hugger since around first grade (and neither has Millie), but after I looked through the notebook, I reached out and gave her hand a little squeeze. She knew what it meant. She squeezed back.

**Four things that broke my trance over the notebook**

------------------------------------------------------------------------

1. The doorbell ringing

2. The phone ringing

3. Ted saying, "Geez, it's the whole town!"

4. Mom calling up the stairs, "Annie, can you come down here, please?"

**Eight people Millie and I found waiting at the bottom of the stairs**

-----------------------------------------------------------------

1. Zora

2. Kate

3. Amelia

4. Charlie

5. Zach

6. Mr. Allbright

7. Nurse Taylor

8. Principal Wilson, who said, "We just wanted to stop by and congratulate our famous student!"

I wasn't sure what to say, but it didn't really matter, because just then Dad came in and said, "That was Channel Seven on the phone. They want to interview you for a story on tonight's *News at Six*."

**Eight questions people had then**

---

1. Zora: What are you going to wear?

2. Amelia: Do you want to borrow my clover outfit for this? You should look more clovery. You're a Clover Gapper now. (I was right! It is Clover Gapper!)

3. Kate: Can you get the weather guy's autograph for me?

4. Ted: Can Mind the Gap play in the background?

5. Mr. Allbright: Do you know that if they ask you about anything that you don't want them to put on air, you should say "off the record" before you answer?

6. Millie (in a whisper): Who are all these people?

7. Dad: Do you think you want to do this, Annie?

8. Me: Should I do it? What would I say?

And then Mom said exactly what I should have known she would say, which was: "It's totally up to you, hon. But I think you'd be great. Just be you."

**What does it mean for me to just be me? Who is that? Ten possible answers**

1. A fifth-grade kid who just found a six-leaf clover

2. A kid who usually notices *a lot*, but only found the clover because it was beside a Frisbee

3. A city kid who accidentally told a family secret

4. A Clover Gapper who is figuring out how to fit in

5. A little sister

6. The quiet friend who only talks if she really has to (and I guess in a news interview, you really have to)

7. The girl who saved Amelia from becoming a blood sister

8. The girl who put Hope in her place at Clover Fest

9. Someone who was really missed by Millie

10. A kid who's just figuring out how to speak up

*Okay, Annie, you got this,* I thought. "Sure," I said. "I'll do it."

**Crowd reaction to my decision**

1. Cheering

2. Laughing at the cheering, which seemed a bit over the top (me and Kate)

3. Hugs (from Mom and Dad)

4. Drumming (from Ted, of course)

5. A little hug from Nurse Taylor, who said she and Mr. Allbright had to go but she would be sure to watch that night

"Why are they leaving together?" Kate whispered as Mr. Allbright and Nurse Taylor walked out the door.

"Off the record?" I said. "I think she's his girlfriend."

**Seven ways life has changed since I became the Clover Kid (that's what the lady on the news called me)**

------------------------------------------------------------

1. I got a bunch of free stuff (like clover necklaces, T-shirts, socks—even a little stuffed clover). I've been trying to pass it out to my friends in a way that seems fair. As lifelong Clover Gappers, they're more excited for the stuff than I am. Zora got the necklaces, Kate got the jeans patches, Zach and Charlie got shoelaces, and Amelia got the pencils (round, of course). I did keep the stuffed clover, though; I named it Jade.

2. Mom and Dad go out more. Everyone got to know our family after my famous find, so they started making new friends. Plus, people were so impressed by Dad's recipes at Clover Fest (his clover guacamole won a blue ribbon) that some other parents asked them to join their gourmet dinner club.

3. Mom has been working more. One of the members of the Clover Council found out she was a graphic designer and checked out her website. He liked Mom's portfolio so much that he asked her to design all new stuff for them: stationery, banners, the works. And some other organizations around here are starting to hire her too. She keeps reminding Ted and me that these are civic clubs with limited budgets and it's not like we've hit the jackpot or anything, but I can tell she's happy to have a little extra income.

4. Everyone at school knows who I am now. Even the older kids. The other day Will Garner (sixth grader) said, "Hey, Annie," to me in the hallway, and I thought Amelia was going to faint. (She says he's crazy gorgeous, and she's kind of right.)

5. For the first time ever, there are people I don't know who know *me*. The other day I was at the drugstore with Mom, and a girl I'd never noticed before asked if she could get a selfie with me. That was definitely a first.

6. The more people I get to know, the less afraid I am to talk to them.

7. Now Millie writes to me more than I write to her. But that's not because I'm famous; it's because we're friends again. And I don't write less because I'm mad at her. I'm just busier these days. I don't have one best friend, like I did in Brooklyn, or any "backup" friends, like I thought I needed. They're all just my friends. And the more friends you have, the more stuff you have to do, so my email-writing time is limited.

**Five ways my life has not changed since becoming the Clover Kid**

1. I still have to help wash the dishes every night.

2. Even though Mom has booked more work, we still aren't sure how long Dad's job will last once

the new highway is done. But he seems more at ease about it the longer it goes on. "Government red tape makes these things last forever," he keeps saying. We'll see. But I don't wonder as much as I used to if we're going to move back to Brooklyn. Ted never asks either. No one has said it out loud, but I think we all might be okay with staying here.

3. I still get embarrassed pretty easily. (Let's just say I learned my lesson about saving chewing gum behind my ear; what worked for Violet Beauregarde does not work for me.)

4. Ted still makes fun of me for doing klutzy things. (He has been calling me Chewie or Chewbacca ever since the gum incident.)

5. I still don't have a phone.

## My four favorite chewing-gum flavors

1. Watermelon

2. Grape

3. Wild cherry

4. Strawberry-kiwi

**Three things I admitted to Kate, Zora, and Amelia in the Pond Fort at the beginning of summer break**

1. I'm afraid of bears.

2. I was afraid I wouldn't meet any friends in Clover Gap. ("But you did!" Amelia said.)

3. I have a really good memory, but for weird stuff. ("We kind of figured," Kate said. "Yeah," Zora added. "You've been talking a lot more lately, and you remember the craziest things about people!")

**What happened after I told the truth about my memory**

1. Nothing. Turns out no one thinks it's creepy (except maybe Ted).

**Seven plans I have for the summer**

1. Finish Mom's book challenge so I can FINALLY GET MY EARS PIERCED.

2. Practice my free throws so I can beat Ted in HORSE.

3. Learn how to dive at the town pool.

4. Visit Millie in Brooklyn. (Mom said we can go there for Fourth of July because Millie has an awesome view of the fireworks from the roof of her building. And Ted is all excited to play with his old band and hit his favorite music stores. He

told Marcus he'd bring back some new guitar picks for him.)

5. Help Kate learn her lines for her drama-camp play. She thinks I'll be good at this because of my memory. I tried telling her it doesn't really work that way, but she says I'm still her best bet.

6. Meet with Amelia to write letters to Zora in Jamaica, where she'll be spending a month with her grandparents. Zora said we had to write to her every day, but we told her it would be more like once a week. (I could tell that standing up to Zora was hard for Amelia, but I think she's getting better at it.) Amelia already made stationery for us to use for the letters. It has a little clover and "From $A^2$ to Z" across the top.

7. Go to our family's special beach spot, Wren Island, with Aunt Pen. The other day I got an email from her saying she can't wait to hear all about how things have been going since she saw us at Thanksgiving, and all the adventures I've been having in Clover Gap.

So much has happened this year, I really don't know what to tell her first.

I guess I'd better start making a list.

# ACKNOWLEDGMENTS

## (OR, SOME OF THE WONDERFUL PEOPLE
## WHO HELPED BRING ANNIE TO LIFE)

1. Everyone who first told me I was a writer, starting with my parents: Mary Lou Keim McGinn, who honored my imagination and took dictation on my earliest stories before I could pen them myself; and Howard McGinn, whose encouragement and contagious love of words sparked my childhood writing endeavors.

2. Kevin McGinn, the funniest person I've ever met, one of my great cheerleaders, and certainly the best human to have spent a childhood with. Like Annie, he's an encyclopedia of memories, and I'm so grateful for his willingness to share them. (Hint: He rode his bike into a pit long before she did.)

3. Jane and Samantha McGinn, for their kindness, bookworm solidarity, and enthusiasm through every milestone.

4. All the little tribes who've taken me in, raised me up, and given me great stories over the years. (Here's looking at you, Sanford kids, Lafayette family, *McCall's* girls, and Brooklyn mamas.)

5. The endlessly spirited, generous, and comforting women of my South Orange–Maplewood village. (Really, what would I do without you?)

6. The incredible teachers of Sanford, N.C.; Lafayette College; and the Bank Street College of Education, whose patience and wisdom fostered a passion for literature, an urge to ask questions, and a deep appreciation for good stories.

7. Melissa Walker, dear friend, N.C.-in-N.Y. sister, and writing shaman, who read an early *Annie* draft, wholeheartedly "got it," and spearheaded the search for others who would agree.

8. My amazing agent, Sarah Burnes of the Gernert Company, whose gently incisive questions brought Annie and her world into sharp focus; and her colleague Logan Garrison Savits, whom I can't thank enough for finding and championing this manuscript, and helping to shepherd it along every step of the way.

9. Julia Maguire and the rest of the team at Knopf Books for Young Readers, whose nurturing helped make Annie's story so much more than even I realized it could be. Julia's guidance helped a character, a town, and a writer grow.

10. Emma Smith, whose friendship I treasured long before our love of children's books (and shared writing dreams) cemented it all the more. And "critique group" seems such an inadequate term to describe Emma, Ariel

Bernstein, Ali Bovis, and Katey Howes, whose brilliant insights, creative story solutions, shared writing tribulations, and panda jokes are daily gifts in my email in-box.

11. Rebecca Crane, whose beautiful illustrations capture exactly how Annie looks when I close my eyes and imagine her. I am in awe of her talent.

12. Lucy Louise and Alice Josephine Mahoney, for the countless laughs, hugs, and inspiring revelations you bring me every day. What a wonder to watch you and your sisterhood grow. As I told you when you were babies, I waited my whole life for you (and it was worth it).

13. Whelan Mahoney, still the sunshine of my life. I thank you most.

# WELCOME TO MIDDLE SCHOOL!

COME MEET EVERYONE IN KRISTIN MAHONEY'S NEW NOVEL.

The 47 People You'll Meet in Middle School

Kristin Mahoney

*Dear Louisa,*

*Today was the last day of school before Thanksgiving break. The end of my first few months of sixth grade. Since school started, you've been asking me what middle school is like. And since then, I've been saying things like "It's fine, whatever." I know this is not a helpful answer. I know you are dying to know what to expect when you start at Meridian Middle School in two years. I know I'm supposed to give you the scoop, show you the ropes, hand you the keys (and a bunch of other clichés Mom and Dad used), because I'm your big sister.*

*The truth is, I'm still figuring it out myself. It's only been a few months, and it's hard to respond to questions when you're still working on the answers. And the fact that <u>this</u> particular school year has started out* as the weirdest ever . . . well, that hasn't helped.

But I will say I've had time to reflect on your question over the past couple of days. (You know how you don't really do anything during the last few days of school before a break? That's still true in middle school.) So while the teachers have been showing movies and tidying up their classrooms and the other kids have been passing notes and falling asleep at their desks or doodling on their sneakers, I've been reflecting. (_Reflecting_ is a big thing middle-school teachers are into. You'll see.)

So, what is middle school like, you ask? (And ask, and ask.)

There are a few things I can tell you:

1. It's nothing like elementary school.
2. Lockers are not as exciting as everyone thinks they'll be.
3. You might be on your own without some of your closest friends. Take me and Layla, for example. She's been my best friend since we were three, and all through elementary school at Starling.

*But Starling kids split up for middle school, and just because she lives one street over from us, she has to go to Parkwood Middle School and we have to go to Meridian. So I had to start a new school without my oldest and closest friend.*

4. *You will have no idea where to go. I don't just mean getting lost in the building (although that happens), but you won't know which people to go to, because you won't know who your people are. You may think you will, but you won't. More on that later.*

5. *The time goes by differently. For one thing, you change classes and teachers for each subject, which sounds like it would make the day go faster. But with certain teachers, it actually makes fifty minutes feel like a year. Like, you look at the clock, and then look up at it again about a month later (or so you think), and it has advanced one minute.*

6. *Time passes differently in other ways too. In elementary school, you talk a lot*

*about the seasons: the changing leaves, the snow in winter, the flowers in spring. There's a harvest festival, a Thanksgiving celebration, a winter concert, a spring fair. They have some of that stuff in middle school. But mostly the year passes with people. The people you notice right away. The people you notice much later. The ones who notice you way before you notice them. And vice versa. The people will surprise you. For better and for worse.*

*So the best way to tell you about middle school is to give you a heads-up about the people you'll meet. Sure, some of these might be different for you in a couple of years . . . but this should give you a pretty good idea. Besides, all I can tell you is how it happened for me. So here you go, Lou. These are the people you'll meet in middle school.*

*Love,*
*Augusta*

# 1. The assistant principal

I wish I could tell you that the first person I saw on the first day of school was someone I knew. It was not.

I made Dad drop me off two blocks from school that morning. This was partly because I wasn't sure what the routine was in middle school, and I didn't want to be the only kid whose parent took them right to the front door. But this was *mostly* because Dad's car was in the shop again and—as you may recall from the first day of school, Lou—he had borrowed the radio-station van to drive for a few days. Some people's parents have a clean, fancy company car to drive for work; lucky us that our dad gets a bright green van that actually has WOLD: YOUR FAVORITE OLDIES painted on the side in orange letters. For first-day-of-school arrival? No thank you.

As I rounded the corner by Meridian Middle, I saw

a crowd of kids who were all complete strangers. They also all looked way older than me. And they seemed like they all knew each other. I knew that more than half the kids at Meridian Middle were coming from a different elementary school than ours, but it still seemed like I should know *someone*. I started wondering if I was in the right place.

Turns out, I was not. And apparently I had *I am in sixth grade—please help me* written on my forehead, because a teacher holding a clipboard actually pointed at me and yelled across the heads of the other kids, "You! Glasses! Blue backpack! Sixth grade?"

You wouldn't think that "glasses" and "blue backpack" would be sufficient identifiers. I mean, other kids had glasses and blue backpacks. But I guess this teacher's pointing was laser-sharp, because about a hundred kids turned and looked right at me after he yelled.

"Um, yes?" I answered, almost in a whisper (and still wondering where the heck everyone I knew was).

"What was that?"

"Yes. Sixth," I said, slightly louder.

"Back door!" the teacher yelled. "Didn't your parents get the email?"

By this point the teacher was making his way over, clapping students on the back, saying hello, and telling some of them to spit out their gum. He was wearing a golf shirt with the school logo on it. The shirt strained over his belly and was tucked snugly into his khaki pants. I wondered how he got his shirt to stay tucked so tight, especially with a big belly. Did he buy extra-long shirts?

"Did your parents get the email?" he asked again.

"I'm not sure?" I said. Since the weekend before school started had been one of our weekends at Dad's apartment, it was possible I wasn't operating with complete information. (You know he's not so great about reading emails thoroughly.) I began to wonder what else he'd missed.

"Well," the teacher explained, "this is the eighth-grade entrance. Sixth graders go to the back."

"Oh, okay." That seemed pretty inhospitable to me, making the new kids go to the back door. But I wasn't going to argue. I turned and started walking down the path that wound around to the back of the building.

"Heeey, Little Gus!" I heard someone call. I knew it had to be a kid from our neighborhood, since he was calling me Gus and not Augusta. I turned and, sure enough, there was Rob Vinson, talking to some other eighth-grade boys. Even though Rob is kind of dopey, he's usually an okay kid. He's always been Mom and

Dad's first choice to walk Iris when we're gone on a day trip somewhere, and he was never jerky to us like some of the other older neighborhood boys were. So hearing his familiar voice on the first day of school was simultaneously comforting and embarrassing. (*Why* did he have to call me Little Gus in front of everyone else? Ugh.)

"It's my neighbor!" Rob announced, not that the boys he was with seemed to care.

"What are you doing on this side of the building, Little Gus?" he asked.

"I got the entrance wrong. That teacher told me to go around back," I said, pointing to the man with the super-tight tuck-in.

"That's not a teacher, Gus," Rob said. "That's an assistant principal. Mr. Wyatt. You don't want to tangle with him."

"I didn't tangle with him," I said. "He just told me I had the wrong door."

"Okay, well, watch yourself with that one. If he told you to go to the back door, you'd better go fast. Why are you still standing here?"

"Because you're still talking to me!"

"Nah, you better go, Little Gus!" Rob shooed me away like I was a pesky dog, never mind that he had been the one detaining me.

I rolled my eyes and went around to the back of the building. And that's where I saw all the kids I knew. All the kids whose parents had read the email properly.

That night I got in a fight with Mom because I told her she needed to make sure Dad read his emails all the way through. And I may have said something like "If you guys still lived together, we wouldn't have these problems." And then Mom felt like dirt, and so did I.

I don't know if you remember that fight, Lou, or if you even heard it. You were standing at the kitchen sink making one of your "potions." (This one contained olive oil, flower petals, and dish soap.) It seemed like you were in your own world. Until you announced that the potion was going to be a special doggy-fur conditioner for Iris, and Mom took one look at it and said there was no way you were going to rub olive oil on the dog.

That's when you snapped back into our world and asked what we were talking about, and I just said, "School." That was the first time you asked me to tell you what middle school was like. That was the first time I said, "It's fine, whatever," and went upstairs to my room.

Anyway, now you know a little. Sixth graders go to the back door. And don't tangle with Mr. Wyatt. He was the first person I met in middle school. And unfortunately, I would meet him again.

# 2. The friend you don't recognize because she turned into a whole new person over the summer

I figured that as I rounded the corner to the back of the building, everything would fall into place. I'd be surrounded by people I knew, and middle school would start feeling the way it was supposed to. And for a second, it did. I spotted Jason Cordrey, Mekhai Curry, and a few other boys I'd known since kindergarten. They looked the same, and they were doing just what they always did last year: trying to spin each other around by their backpack straps.

The next person I recognized was Addison Aldrich, standing near a picnic bench with the same pose she'd had every day as she held court during recess in fifth grade: backpack loosely hanging off one shoulder, right leg ramrod straight, and left foot poised on tiptoe, as though the ballet flats she owns in every color were actual toe shoes. Addison and I had never really hit it off. We tried being friends for about five minutes in second grade, but then she dared me to smear peanut butter on Jason Cordrey's pencil. Jason has a bad peanut allergy. I wouldn't do it. Addison called me a chicken, flipped her hair at me, and walked away. Yeah. She was a hair flipper already in second grade. Enough said.

Anyway, on the first day of school Addison was talking to a girl who looked familiar. I figured the girl must be in seventh grade, or even eighth, because she was tall, with huge hoop earrings, and maybe even had a little bit of makeup on? No one I knew in my grade wore makeup yet, not even the girls in Addison's crowd.

I heard someone yell, "Hey, Marcy!" and I looked around. The only Marcy I knew was Marcy Shea. I never told you this, but even though Marcy and I had been friends since first grade, she was kind of bugging me last year. Layla was in a different fifth-grade class, and we weren't allowed to sit with other classes in the cafeteria. So Marcy always had to sit beside me at lunch, put her sleeping bag beside mine at slumber parties, and ask if I would ride on the bus with her on field trips (like a month before the trips even happened, just to make sure there was no chance I'd sit with anyone else). I don't know why it bugged me so much; I'd never minded hanging out with her before. It just felt like at the same time Marcy needed to be together constantly, I started needing to be in my own space more. Not just around Marcy, but with other people too. Mom. Dad. You. (Sorry.)

It was like I didn't just need physical space; I also needed space in my head. For all the things I was starting to wonder about more, like what other people thought of me, and whether my jeans were too short or my laugh was too loud or my water bottle was a stupid color.

I felt like I needed space to think about other things too, specifically all the extra thoughts I was having after Mom and Dad told us they were splitting up. I mean, some of the things they brought up in that conversation were things that never even would have occurred to me, but now they were all I could think about. Like when Mom said, "We want you to know this isn't your fault." Well, yeah. Did you ever for a second think that the divorce was our fault, Lou? I didn't. What could we have done to make our parents get divorced? Sheesh. And when Dad said, "We will find a way to make this work, and you will not have to go to court to choose between us." Ummmm, okay. I never even knew that was a thing that could really happen. But now I was thinking, *Wait . . .* could *that really happen?* And the way Mom laughed nervously and said "Of course not!" after Dad brought it up made me wonder even more.

I don't know about you, but when I am thinking thoughts like *Am I going to have to choose between my parents in court?* or even *Why am I the only one in this class with an orange water bottle?,* it makes me feel— I don't know—prickly. And if someone grabs my arm and says "Sit beside me on the bus!" while I'm quietly wondering if I'm to blame for my parents' divorce, well . . . sometimes it's all I can do not to jerk my arm away and yell, "Sit by yourself!"

But I never did that. As much as Marcy annoyed me, I was never very good at saying no to her (even in a less dramatic way), so we wound up beside each other at a lot of lunches and slumber parties, and on a lot of field-trip buses. Her family was going to be away in Nova Scotia for most of the summer, and I was relieved to be getting a break from her.

On the last day of fifth grade, Marcy had told me we had to "strategize" for the first day of middle school. She said she'd call me when she got back from her vacation so we could coordinate our outfits, transportation, and arrival time for the first day. I was a little surprised when I never heard from her, but mostly I felt like I'd dodged a clingy bullet. For all I knew, she'd moved to Canada for good.

So on the first day of school, when a kid hollered "Marcy," the last person I expected to respond was the tall, lipstick-wearing, hoop-earringed girl talking to Addison. But sure enough, it was her. I could see it now. Under the makeup and between the hoop earrings, her face was a longer, narrower version of the Marcy who'd plunked her lunch box down beside mine every day in the cafeteria last year.

"Hey, girl!" Marcy yelled to the kid who'd called her name, raising skyward an arm full of bangle bracelets that were only a little bigger than her giant hoop earrings.

She noticed me standing there as her arm came back down and said, "Oh—hey, Augusta," in a voice that was suddenly way less enthusiastic.

Before I could even say hi back, Addison grabbed Marcy's arm and inspected one of the bangle bracelets. "Ooh!" she squealed. "Is this the one you got the day we went whale-watching?"

"You guys went whale-watching together?" I asked.

"Yes!" Addison squealed again. "This year Marcy's family summered in the same spot where my family always summers. We went on a whale-and-dolphin watch together."

"You *summered* there, huh?" Louie, I know you (and Mom, and Dad) always hate my sarcastic tone, but this was ridiculous. Who uses "summer" as a verb? And twice in the same sentence?

"Yes. We *spent the summer* there. *Summered,*" Marcy explained, like I was an idiot. "My parents say we can go back every year now."

"We summered here in Meridian," a voice behind me said. "My parents say we'll do that every year too." I turned and saw Nick Zambrano spinning a Frisbee on his index finger. Marcy rolled her eyes and turned back around.

"Hey, Gus," Nick said. "Thought I was gonna be late this morning. My parents didn't read the email and I went to the front door."

I said hi back to Nick, but I was too distracted to really pay attention to him. With her new long legs and made-up face and "summering" in Nova Scotia, Marcy looked like a different kind of creature from the rest of us. *Do I seem any different from last year?* I wondered. This was something I couldn't really get a handle on: how I came off to other people. (That was another thing I was sometimes wondering about when I felt like

I needed space: What kind of person did I seem like?) I tried quickly glancing down at myself to see if I looked that different from last year. I had new sneakers. My hair was a little longer. That was about it. Nothing like the new-and-improved Marcy.

I know what you're thinking, Louie: *That couldn't happen to any of* my *friends!* Trust me. It will. In fact, from your crew of kids, my money's on Isabella. Look how much she's changed already since kindergarten, when she used to cry at drop-off every morning. Now she plays travel lacrosse, and she spent the summer at cheerleading camp. Mark my words: On the first day of sixth grade, you may not know who she is.